THE
LAST SCAM

JEAN REZAB

COPYRIGHT

PROLOGUE

Braden glanced around the restaurant before his gaze returned to the table where Rory and Jade sat across from him. They'd already started eating, but his stomach rebelled at the thought of food. Or coffee. Or water.

He'd planned on a quieter setting to discuss the situation, not a noisy Mexican restaurant where he had to scream to be heard above the music. Getting together at the restaurant was the solution offered by the others. At the inn, they needed the supplies he picked up in Dickinson.

As they ate, he wished Lauren had come to share the news she'd discovered. "Lauren told me Phil is going to be staying at the Crocus Hill Inn in a few weeks. Someone sent him a blackmail text to get him there."

Forks clattered as they looked up from their food.

"What are you talking about?" Jade tossed back her dark hair streaked with bright pink. She scowled at Braden before turning to Rory. "Did you send the text to Phil?"

How badly did Rory want the money Phil scammed from him? Braden had about enough of their group, and these two were the hardest to handle. At least the others balanced the situation when they were around. "Lauren told me the text threatened Phil. If he didn't show up at the Crocus Hill Inn, the sender would go to the police with evidence of his investment scheme."

Rory continued eating his king-sized burrito during the announcement and stopped long enough to throw in his two cents. "Lauren told us last time we met that Phil already knows we've been to the police with evidence. I gave the detective everything I signed when Phil talked me into investing in his scheme. That alone should be enough to put him on trial. Why would he go to the inn? He has nothing to gain."

"According to Lauren, he intends to find out who sent the text so he can get revenge. Do you think I want him as a guest where I work? This sucks." Braden picked up his glass of water and drank through the straw until the sound of sucking indicated emptiness. Time to get back to the inn. His boss, Courtney, wanted to make sure they'd sent the right flooring for the enclosed sunroom, and he had a forty-five-minute drive with the flooring in the back of the truck.

Rory turned to Jade, squinting at her through his half-closed eyes. "You haven't denied sending the text. Did you?"

"Of course not. What purpose would that serve?"

"Who knows with you? You're bent on revenge." The burrito a mere memory, he scraped up the rest of the rice and cleaned his plate.

"Phil's going to the inn, and I'm in Dickinson. How can I get revenge on him out there in neverland? It would be easier if he'd stay in

Minot, where there are more people to blend with the crowd." She picked the last of the spicy shrimp out of its bed of rice and nibbled.

Rory shoved his chair back from the table. "Why don't we all go out there to stay? We can try to get our money back."

Shuddering, Braden shook his head. "No. I work there, man. We don't need everyone gathering at the inn. With my background, you know how hard it is for me to find work. Since Phil scammed Mom out of money, I need a job more than ever."

He didn't plan to tell the group he spent time in prison for his own activities as a thief. Trying to justify he stole for a good cause backfired in a hurry. The courts disagreed, and he came to realize they were right. His employers knew the truth, and Alex even shared that he had spent time in prison to help a friend avoid prosecution. His friend was the guilty party, but he had cancer, so Alex took the blame—a nobler purpose than Braden's reason for his time behind bars.

"I disagree with Braden." Having finally finished the shrimp, Jade set her fork on her plate. "If we all go out there, we could show strength in numbers. He'd realize his scheming days are over."

Braden's stomach continued to churn. "Nothing good can come from going out to the inn, and it's not fair. I need my job."

"It's a good idea." Jade gave Rory a challenging stare. "How about it?"

His face lit up. "Yeah. Let's do it. I'm going to talk the others into coming along."

Braden groaned, hoping the others would have more common sense and decide not to come to the inn. "I hope there aren't any rooms available."

He would rush back to the inn and warn Courtney and Alex to tell everyone they were booked up. What excuse could he give? They needed the inn full of paying guests. Should he tell his bosses the truth? He hadn't told them about his mother being scammed by Phil.

What a nightmare. His first job out of prison had turned into a plot to drive him crazy. "If you're going to go, you'll have to follow the program. This is no run-of-the-mill bed and breakfast. When you tell them you're coming—if they have an opening—they'll want you to share what part of your life you want to reset. The program involves focusing on a personal problem you're having, Bible study, psychologist visits, and group therapy. It's called 'A New Day.'"

"What?" Rory's face lost color. "I'm not sure about that." He looked back at Jade.

She shrugged. "I'm going. Make something up. You do what you want."

Braden knew if Jade went, Rory would go. No way would he lose the opportunity to get his money back, especially if Jade made it a competition. How had this group started, anyway? Lauren was the first group member he met.

He'd walked up the sidewalk to Phil's house, and Lauren came out the front door, passing him. "If you're here to get your money back, don't bother. He won't budge. He's total scum."

At the venom in her voice, Braden had stopped on the sidewalk. His brain finally caught up to the fact she knew something, and he rushed after her. "What do you mean?"

She stopped and took a good look at him. "It's not your money. You don't look like you have any."

What did she see when she looked at him? "He stole my mom's money."

"Well, don't expect to get it back." She turned around and left him floundering in multiple conflicting thoughts.

Should he try and get Phil to return the money? He shook his head to clear it and retraced his way to the front door. Ten minutes later, he left without the money and no doubt in his mind the woman had Phil pegged. He was scum.

The woman had stood by her car, waiting for him, and she introduced herself as Lauren. After that, they met regularly to discuss what to do about the situation. Then Jade appeared. Eventually Melanie, Skylar, and Rory and his wife, Ivy, joined.

Now, here he sat with Jade and Rory, meeting in Dickinson because he needed to be here today, and only a few of them could make it.

What would Lauren say when he told her the whole group intended to gather around Phil like vultures to get their money and their relatives' money back? She'd be at the inn too.

And what should he tell his bosses, Courtney and Alex, about the guests arriving at their new Crocus Hill Inn in two weeks? Should he tell the detective what the group planned to do? Was it illegal? His head began to ache.

Would the others in the group book rooms at the inn too? If Phil intended to come, what was his purpose? He knew they'd given information to the police. Did he have his own agenda?

CHAPTER 1
Two Weeks Later

Courtney peered out of the office window at the large black SUV coming up their long driveway. All morning she'd been praying the week would turn out okay. She turned to Alex. "I wonder who our first guest is."

He glanced up from his desk with a grin. "Our first guest or guests. Crocus Hill Inn is officially in business!"

She continued to stare out the window. A couple who appeared to be in their fifties emerged from the black vehicle. Clad in a pink plaid shirt with jeans and sneakers, the frowning woman wore sunglasses matching her short brown hair. She slammed the passenger door closed.

The man's hair was thinning, and his cleanly shaven face bore a similar frown as his wife's. He wore a tan polo shirt with his jeans and boots. The boots appeared new, even from this distance. Scanning the house and the prairie countryside, his mouth twisted into a snarl.

Courtney's stomach churned and twisted into a knot. Maybe breakfast was a mistake. What had she brought on herself with this program? Was this God's plan for her life? "I don't believe I can do this."

Alex walked over and gave her a reassuring hug. "There's no need to worry. Everything will turn out fine. They'll be nervous too. This isn't exactly a regular bed-and-breakfast scenario this week. It's a retreat. People come to reset their lives. Remember our motto, 'A New Day.' We're going to assist these people as much as we can and leave the results to God."

"You're right." She squeezed his hand, her stomach partially settled. Alex walked this path with her. She'd dreamed of the kind of inn where they'd help people, and the time had come. "Let's go greet our guests. At least we'll have Clarissa available tomorrow to put people at ease. Thank goodness we made a deal with them to co-own this place and counsel our guests through the summer months."

Courtney and Alex decided to have their joint office face the driveway before it curved around to the parking area, which gave them the advantage of a first glance at their guests. Guests who appeared to be starting out their week with a fight.

Alex followed her out of the office, his hand warm on her shoulder. They stepped out the front door.

Courtney started down the front steps, calling out to them, "Welcome to the Crocus Hill Inn. Would you like help with your luggage?" They walked over to the couple's vehicle where the man stood.

"That would be good." The guy's irritated voice inspired another silent prayer.

She held out her hand. "Hi. I'm Courtney, and this is my husband, Alex."

The man had a firm handshake. "I'm Phil Young. You're a little far away from a big town, aren't you?" He frowned.

Courtney took a step back, her welcoming smile pinned to her face. Why did the couple drive to the country if he preferred a city? "It's about three miles to Elm City, which has a small grocery store, and you can get gasoline and a few other things. Dickinson is about a half-hour drive at the most, and it has a lot more to offer if you're looking for city life. We have access to everything we need here."

"You must be Kristina." Alex held out his hand to the woman as she joined them.
She moved her glasses to the top of her hair like a headband and met his gaze. After quickly shaking his hand, she lowered her sunglasses. "You can call me Kris. Everyone does."

"Thank you," Alex said easily.

Courtney considered Phil's attitude. Despite the fact he knew the inn was out of town, he came anyway. The couple's stated their reason for attending A New Day Program was to work on their marriage, and it didn't take a genius to see problems between them. "Where's your luggage? We'll get you settled in your room. I'm sure after your drive from Montana, you must be ready to rest."

"Actually, I'm looking forward to a cold soda and a walk around the grounds. This is great." Kris smiled for the first time as she gazed around the place. "I love the country. The hill over on the other side of the road is gorgeous with all those purple crocuses, and I love the old shed at the top. The open prairie is nice compared to trees blocking the view."

"It's been ten years since you've seen anything except sidewalks and concrete driveways." Phil's mouth twisted in a sneer.

"You wanted to come here." She shrugged at Courtney, who took it to mean *Men—who can understand their whims?*

Nothing added up. Phil complained, but he convinced Kris to come to the inn. *If they are so miserable, why did they come?*

Phil grabbed the biggest bag and picked it up. "The shed might be rustically interesting and the flowers pretty, but you've forgotten the bad parts about the country."

"In the spring, there are no bad parts." Kris threw out her arms to indicate the area.

Cheered by Kris's enthusiasm, Courtney appreciated the landscaping they'd managed to complete, along with the natural beauty of the crocuses.

She and Alex debated names for the two-story inn for a long time. They had remembered when Gary showed them the property, and in the fall had decided on Crocus Hill Inn and painted the inn the color of crocuses. They'd decided on some green bushes for each side of the steps into the inn and a few evergreens in the back yard.

They walked up the steps with the luggage. "You picked a good time to come. The end of April is warm enough to enjoy a walk, and the bugs haven't made much of an appearance yet. We've got a cold soda, and you can wander wherever you want." Alex opened the front door.

***

Courtney's initial nervousness disappeared as she went about showing the Youngs the great room, which she and Alex named the entry into their inn. They decided to have an open concept with a dining table, a kitchenette, and a large section big enough to seat thirty people, which they called the great room. Several different groupings of furniture gave the room a cozy vibe. They included a place for board or card games.

The kitchenette was large enough to prepare quick snacks. Willow would make their meals in the main kitchen in the next room.

About fifteen minutes after Courtney showed Phil and Kris their room, a king bed with an attached bathroom, Kris chose a soda from the options in the kitchenette and headed outside for her walk.

Phil refused to join her and sat in the main great room. Courtney watched as he relaxed in the navy recliner with a book. From the title, he'd chosen a spy novel.

Settling down at the dining room table, she gazed out the window at the beautiful purple crocuses and green grass stretching for miles. The sun shone on the table where she sat sipping from a bottle of water. Enjoying the warmth as she waited for the next guests, she pondered the situation between Phil and Kris.

They already disagreed over the location of the getaway. If Phil continued to grouse about the distance from a town, he probably liked the nightlife. The only place open near them at night was the small-town bar in Elm City a few miles away.

Courtney had only been there with Alex a few times. Once, they arrived in town and needed something quick to eat. The bar served appetizers in the evening. The second time, they'd finally chosen the name of the inn and decided to celebrate.

The bar's open hours needed to be researched. She'd better make up a cheat sheet of the nearby towns, the distances to reach them, and the amenities in each town. Another thing to add to her never-ending to-do list.

She and Alex had owned Crocus Hill Inn for about eight months and spent all their time renovating the building and as much of the grounds as they could before winter. They'd moved from a small house they'd been renting in Elm City in early spring. Their apartment above the inn was ready for them to move at that point, so Courtney could pursue her dream of helping people. They'd been lucky to find experienced contractors in the area who wanted the work on the inside of the inn during the winter months to supplement their income.

Thanks to the grant coming through, and the loan from Clarissa and Hugh, they'd been able to proceed faster than anticipated. Maybe the anxiety came from the fear something would go wrong.

After what happened during the renovation, she knew how fast everything could change.

When they completely booked for this first trial week, she'd been happily surprised. Maybe Phil was upset because he didn't want to make life changes, despite the fact he made plans to come, instead of Kris. Answers would come as the week progressed.

They advertised Crocus Hill Inn's A New Day program as a retreat with group discussion time, psychologist appointments, Bible studies, and free time to relax and consider making life changes. But Phil didn't seem to have the mindset for the program.

The sound of tires on gravel caught her attention. A small red hatchback rumbled into the driveway. She caught a glimpse of a dark-haired woman wearing sunglasses. Hopefully a more upbeat guest. At least Phil and Kris wouldn't dominate her thoughts anymore.

CHAPTER 2

Courtney reached the front door of the house at the same time a car door slammed. She stepped outside and greeted the young woman, who removed her sunglasses. Her clear blue gaze studied Courtney.

"Hi. My name is Lauren Mazour." She started talking before Courtney could greet her.

"Hi, Lauren. I'm Courtney Richmond. Welcome to Crocus Hill Inn. Would you like help with your luggage?"

"I'm fine." Lauren waved her away. "Only one suitcase. I'm used to traveling light."

"Oh. Do you travel often?" Courtney always overpacked.

"I'm a writer. I like to research the settings of my stories." She opened the back driver's side door and pulled out a suitcase and a black backpack she slung over her left shoulder.

"Sounds interesting. I'd love to hear more about your writing this week. Are you going to write about this part of the state?" At least Lauren appeared like she wanted to be here.

"I haven't decided yet." She looked around. "It depends if inspiration hits here. The scenery is beautiful."

"Most people either like it or hate it. Come on in and have a drink of something cold or hot. We have tea, coffee, soda, and water. Your preference." She started walking to the stairs.

A smile lit Lauren's face. "Great. I'll take some water. I'm parched."

At least one of their guests seemed to have a sunny disposition.

They entered the inn, and Lauren studied the space, her gaze settling on the games set up on the far side of the room. She dropped her suitcase and backpack by the door. "Backgammon. It's been forever since I've played. Maybe someone else is interested and remembers the rules."

"I believe my husband, Alex, knows how to play. There will likely be at least one other person." Courtney followed her over to the games area.

Lauren surveyed the other tables. One was piled with board games. A table in the corner displayed old-fashioned hand-held electronic games, like Yahtzee and poker. A chess board was laid out and ready to go. She stood there tossing a pawn in her hand before setting it back down.

Looking around the rest of the room, she took in Phil reading his book. She raised a brow at Courtney, who shrugged.

Phil didn't glance at them, much less appear interested in introductions. He'd probably already snuck a peek. Mentally blocking him, she turned to Lauren. "Let me get you a bottle of water, and I'll show you to your room. You can explore more inside and out at your leisure."

While Lauren went back to the entrance and picked up her belongings, Courtney got her two bottles of water from the fridge. She led Lauren down the long hallway.

"You're in Room 6." Courtney stopped at the second-to-last room at the end of the hallway. "The rooms on the left are staff rooms, and the rooms on the right are the guests' rooms. Let Alex or myself know if you need anything."

When Courtney slid the keycard through the slot and opened the door, Lauren exclaimed in delight. "This is perfect. You even have a table with chairs where I can set up my laptop and write. And you've put it in front of the south window." She laughed. "I'm in trouble. I'm going to stare outside too often and avoid writing."

"You can always sit in one of the stuffed armchairs with your laptop if you prefer a different view. Plus, the afternoon sunlight might force you to move the table away from the window or close the blinds."

"We'll see." Lauren set her suitcase and backpack on the table.

"If you ever want to escape to your room for a meal, you can always dish up in the other room and come back here to eat."

"I do eat at odd times because of my writing. If I'm getting the words written, I don't want to stop. I'll be fine. Like I said, I'm used to traveling."

Courtney handed her the room keycard and walked over to the door. "Enjoy your stay. There's a button by the door if you need something in the middle of the night. It only rings in Alex and my room, so you won't be disturbing anyone else."

She opened the door and stepped into the hallway. "Let me know if there's anything you need."

Lauren spun in a circle and stopped when she faced the door. Her eyes radiated happiness. "I've got everything I could possibly want. Thank you."

Courtney closed the door, breathing a silent sigh of relief and thanks to God for Lauren. In the great room, Phil remained immersed in his book. She went to the office to talk with Alex, keying in the code for the door before entering.

Alex glanced up from his papers. His dark brown hair stood on end in the front from running his hands through it. "How's it going out there?"

"I don't know. Okay, I guess." The butterflies in her stomach finally settled.

Alex walked over to where she stood in front of the window, put his hands on her shoulders and rubbed lightly. "Tension here."

The warmth of his fingers soothed her, and her shoulders relaxed a few inches. She leaned against him. "Thanks. This is harder than I thought it would be."

His hands dropped from her shoulders, and he hugged her, his chin resting on the top of her head. "You're a strong woman, Courtney Richmond. I'd bet on you any day. It's only natural meeting all these people would be stressful."

"Thanks." She turned and hugged him back, cocooned in his arms. "Has anyone told you you're a wonderful husband?"

"My wife occasionally mentions it."

She smiled against his chest, smelling the fresh scent of soap on his skin and shirt. "She'll have to mention it more often."

"Her husband wouldn't mind." He laughed.

She took a step back. "Thanks, Husband."

"You're welcome."

"Can I ask a favor?" Courtney fiddled with the button on his plaid shirt.

"Sure."

She looked up at him. "Can you stay with me the rest of the day? Just for this first group?"

He pulled her into a tight hug this time. "Definitely. This grant documentation can wait for the weekend. The committee doesn't require the forms until the end of the month."

"Thanks. I'll help you with it over the weekend." She hugged him closer for a moment and stepped back when she heard tires on gravel.

She handed him a mirror she kept in her desk drawer. "We have more guests. You might want to fix your hair in the front."

He took the mirror and smoothed the strands into place.

From the window, she caught a glimpse of Kris returning from her walk. She stopped to chat with a young woman in a lime-green jacket and a short blunt cut of dark hair. It looked dyed black from this distance.

Courtney saw a few more cars coming up the driveway. Her heartbeat slowed, and she felt ready to continue the adventure. "Yep. We're on. More guests."

"I'm with you all the way." He squeezed her hand and shut down his computer. As he followed her out of the office, the door closed and locked automatically.

***

The next few hours blurred with the activity of greeting the rest of their guests and getting them settled. Most of them lingered a while in their rooms before returning to the great room.

Courtney and Alex served an evening buffet meal at 6:00 p.m. for everyone interested. Two carts beside the island held all the dishes and utensils. All the guests filed along the center island, ladling steaming creamy potato bacon soup into dark blue Fiestaware bowls.

Everyone seemed to find the options to their liking, because there were a lot of satisfied smiles and comments as they tasted the potato soup, homemade bread, and salad.

Alex and Courtney stood, and Courtney started her prepared speech. "Please let us know if you need anything else. Let's go around the table and introduce ourselves. You'll have plenty of time this week to become better acquainted."

"I'm Alex, and this is Courtney." Alex held Courtney's hand. "We're from the small town of Chokecherry Valley, North Dakota, and moved to western North Dakota to open this inn as a dream project about eight months ago. We sent you the list of events for the week. If you didn't get a copy, let me know.

"As we emailed you, the program is beginning this week, and we're concentrating on counseling only. We'll implement the full program in the fall. We meet at 10:00 a.m. at the dining table to discuss the program completely. Your appointment tomorrow afternoon with Dr. Clarissa Alois will be your first individual planned event. After everyone has introduced themselves, you're free to do as you please this evening."

He motioned to Phil, who sat next to him. "Let's start introductions on this side of the table and go around." He motioned clockwise.

"I'm Phil." A scowl returned to his face.

Courtney nearly groaned out loud. They should have started with a happier guest.

As they went around the table, Kris gave her name and enthused about her enjoyment of a walk in the fresh country air.

Lauren introduced herself by saying, "I write."

"Anything we've ever heard of?" Phil asked.

Courtney's mouth turned down before she reminded herself he was a guest and made the effort to come to the inn for help.

"Not unless you like romances or travel books. Have you traveled much?" Lauren studied Phil.

"A little." A smile crossed his face, the first Courtney saw since he arrived.

She'd remember traveling might be a potential conversation starter with him. Her phone had a notes app she should learn to use. She also noted Lauren could defuse his irritation.

The young woman beside Lauren spoke up next. "I'm Melanie." Her reddish-brown hair shone under the overhead light. She gave a shy smile. "I have a young daughter, Sylvia, and I'm an accountant."

"We should have plenty to talk about." Alex caught her gaze. "I'm an accountant too. Braden is learning some of the spreadsheets and other boring things."

Braden anxiously scanned the group. "I'm the groundskeeper here at Crocus Hill. As soon as I have the backyard ready for the wedding, and the wedding is over, then I'll concentrate on those spreadsheets in earnest."

"If I can ask," Lauren hesitated, "who's getting married? You can tell me it's none of my business."

Alex smiled. "It's fine. You're all sharing personal information, and this is a semi-public event anyway. My brother, Paul, is getting married at the inn in two weeks."

"Oh." Lauren nodded. "Cool."

"Right," Phil muttered.

The young lady with a black bob haircut streaked with pink strands spoke up. "I'm sure you'll throw a wonderful wedding for them. I'm Jade. Here to soak up spring sunshine and sightsee."

The guy at the end of the table jumped in, "We're Rory and Ivy."

He couldn't have looked more unlike his wife as he overshadowed her petite frame and her beautiful shoulder-length pale-blond hair. Rory looked like a former high school football player.

They appeared to be in their younger thirties, as did most of the people at the table, except Phil and Kris. Interesting. Courtney would have thought they would see more people in their late forties to their sixties, like Phil and Kris, who wanted a fresh start.

Everyone followed Phil's example of not volunteering where they lived.

"Thanks for introducing yourselves." Courtney sat down, and Alex joined her. "Willow is our cook, and Skylar is our housekeeper. We also have a psychologist, Dr. Clarissa Alois, whom you all have appointments with tomorrow. Her husband, Deacon Hugh Alois, will lead the Bible studies once we start offering them in the fall. They live and practice in Elm City during the times they aren't working here. They happen to be visiting relatives in Bismarck this weekend, or they'd be here this evening. You'll meet them tomorrow.

"You're free to ask for additional appointments with Clarissa if you want to discuss something. Deacon Hugh has a theological degree and has taken classes in counseling also, so anything spiritual you'd like to discuss, he'd be happy to help.

"The schedule is up on the bulletin board." Alex pointed to a spot in the games area, where a corkboard hung on the wall with papers pinned there. "Phone numbers are listed for Courtney, me, Hugh, and Clarissa, so you can make appointments by calling or stopping us in the hallway. Courtney and I'll be around most of the time, and our office is the third door down the hallway on the opposite side from the guest rooms. Just knock.

"Did I cover everything?" he asked Courtney.

She nodded. When he took over the explanations, warmth flowed through her chest. The initial excitement of the day sapped her strength. She'd been thinking about each person's reason for being at the inn and what they wanted to accomplish.

When reserving their room, a short questionnaire asked them for the issue they'd come to the inn to address in the A New Day program. She was only a cog in the wheel, arranging for these people to see Clarissa and Hugh. God would lead the guests to a breakthrough, if that was His plan. If only one of their guests made a breakthrough, the week would be a success.

"We only have the one television in the room off the great room," Alex said. "Please keep the door closed when you're watching to keep the noise level down in the rest of this area. Thank you for coming to our inn and being our guests. We hope you'll enjoy your week here. Now, let's enjoy the rest of the meal Willow prepared."

They tucked into their food. Desultory conversations floated around the table, as those sitting beside each other volunteered slightly more information than their brief introductions. Courtney didn't know why, but she sensed an underlying tension among her guests. Phil wore his perennial sneer. Melanie avoided eye contact. Lauren seemed distracted. And Jade's fingers fluttered around like butterflies taking wing as they talked to each other. Everyone ate quickly and went their separate ways.

Courtney felt they couldn't get away from each other fast enough. Maybe they were nervous about their appointments with Clarissa, or they were a large group of introverts. She needed to ask Alex if he had the same impression.

CHAPTER 3

Phil settled in the recliner next to the couch and took the book he'd been reading earlier from the end table beside his chair. He read, ignoring everyone around him. He and Kris avoided each other.

Jade—Courtney thought of her as the girl with the pink highlights—joined Lauren on the couch. When she arrived, she'd scrutinized Courtney's face when telling her she'd traveled from northern North Dakota. Courtney couldn't figure out why it mattered to Jade. Getting a conversation going with her might give her an answer.

Sitting on the armchair near the couch where Jade and Lauren slumped in comfort, she smiled to keep them at ease. "Jade, you mentioned you haven't been to this part of the state. What are you hoping to see while you're here?"

Returning the smile, Jade straightened. "I want to see the Badlands. They look dark and foreboding from a distance. It's all those shadows where the hills hide the sun. I want to see it up close."

"You sound like an artist." Courtney enjoyed sharing information about the area and glanced at Lauren, including her in the conversation. She was listening to Courtney and Jade.

"From a distance, the hills appear formidable," Courtney agreed. "There's a road you can follow at this time of year. Unfortunately, some of the tourist attractions aren't open until after Memorial Day. The visitor's center in Medora has an online guide and a phone number to call if you need to confirm which scenic roads you can use."

Jade turned her smile on Phil. "I checked out the online guide. I wanted to see the Medora Musical, but the program doesn't begin until June. Maybe I'll come back another time."

Phil put down his book and stared at Jade. Although the discussion of sightseeing in the Badlands wasn't a scintillating subject, he'd found something or, rather, someone more interesting than his book.

He watched as the three of them continued discussing the possible sights in the area. Whenever Jade spoke, he joined the conversation with an observation or question. She swung her short hair back, pink strands flying, and smiled directly at him.

Kris gripped her coffee cup at this display, focusing on Phil. Her glare in his direction intensified as the discussion continued.

Courtney turned to Lauren. "Would you like to see anything in particular?"

Lauren glanced up from studying her fingernails, which she suddenly found interesting when Jade and Phil began flirting. "Nowhere specific. I like driving around the countryside. I've noticed many prairie roses and crocuses. I've seen a deer or two. I'm happy wandering and discovering surprises."

"Enjoy the scenery. It is amazing how far away you can see on the prairie." Courtney stood up when Lauren nodded and studied her nails again.

The show between Jade and Phil put a damper on her mood. Time to talk to Melanie and then settle into the apartment upstairs for the night. Alex was outside with Braden, Rory, and Ivy. While it was only 8:00 p.m., the guests didn't need a babysitter. Maybe they'd relax if she left.

Courtney walked over and observed Melanie playing the battery-operated Yahtzee game. She appeared content by herself. "You can take the game to your room if you'd be more comfortable."

Melanie glanced up and smiled. "It's nice hearing other people talk around me. I'm okay here. I got my quiet time on the drive."

"Great." Courtney smiled in return.

She walked outside and, after a few words with the guests, told Alex she would be upstairs for the rest of the evening. Alex stayed with the others, who decided to take an evening walk, as the light outside didn't fade until around 9:00 p.m.

After saying goodnight to the guests in the great room, she went to the three-bedroom apartment upstairs where she and Alex lived. They'd split the upstairs into two apartments, so when they had personal guests, their friends and family could stay. One ran the length of the north side of the building, and theirs stretched across the south side of the second floor.

Tomorrow would come soon enough. She'd have a better idea how to run the A New Day Program as she observed the guests interacting. Maybe they should have put the entire program into effect right away. *Am I giving my guests enough guidance with the program?* They could do whatever suited them unless she scheduled group sessions.

Right now, she'd review the reasons they'd given for coming to the inn while she waited for Alex. By the end of the week, she'd be ready for a break, but her dream had come true. Crocus Hill Inn was open for business.

Remembering Kris's blank expression as she watched the laughing interaction between Jade and Phil, Courtney felt a twinge of unease slide down her spine. What was Kris thinking while Jade flirted with Phil? He'd finally spoken to his fellow guests—well, Jade anyway. Why her?

Yes, tomorrow should be interesting.

CHAPTER 4
Monday

Cinnamon invaded Courtney's dreams, and she woke with a satisfied groan. Willow's list of breakfasts included cinnamon rolls this morning. She glanced at the clock beside the bed. 5:00 a.m. She had another half hour before her alarm sounded, but she knew she wouldn't be able to go back to sleep.

Alex read the Bible on his side of the bed. His reading light faced away from her but illuminated the page of the book.

"Good morning."

He turned to her with a smile. "Good morning. You slept soundly."

"You mean I snored." She bumped his side with her elbow.

"Right."

She swung her feet over the side of the bed and turned on the overhead light. "I'm ready to get going for the day. How about you?"

He looked down at his book. "About five more minutes."

"Don't hurry. We have time. I'm going to shower." She left him to his prayers and enjoyed a hot shower.

By the time she dressed, he'd finished his shower and stood in front of the bathroom mirror, shaving.

She watched from the bathroom doorway. "I'm going to go see if Willow needs help. I'll join you in the office if she doesn't. Is there something you want from the kitchen?"

"My usual coffee. I'll join the earlier guests for a roll and some eggs later."

Courtney nodded. "We might have to exercise more if we keep eating like our guests."

"The guests will keep us busy enough. At least no one needed anything last night. The bell didn't ring." He set his razor on the counter. "I appreciated the break."

Courtney frowned. "I'm getting weird vibes from these guests. There's an underlying tension, and I feel something bad is going to happen."

Alex wiped his face and joined her in the bedroom. His brown eyes reflected her worry. "What's going on? I didn't notice anything."

"Phil irritated Kris because he enjoyed Lauren's and Jade's company last evening. They joked around, and she sat watching with a blank expression, not contributing to the conversation. Creepy.

"And a few small things. Jade started to say something when she introduced herself. When she caught Lauren watching her, she changed what she planned to say. I feel like they know each other, but why would they hide it from us?" Courtney tried to remember the other thing that hadn't made sense, but the memory didn't return.

"Maybe the introductions bored Lauren," he suggested.

"I don't think so. She focused on each of their comments. It probably doesn't matter. If they know each other, it will come out eventually. I guess I'm worried and letting my imagination roam because this is our trial opening week."

He hugged her and then held her away from him, staring into her eyes. "It's first-time jitters. You'll be fine as the week progresses. We're getting into the rhythm of owning an inn.
You're concerned because of the promise to help them with counseling and time to work on their problems instead of the usual bed-and-breakfast places where people usually vacation. This is more than a vacation for them. They're trying to make life decisions, and we don't know what those decisions may be. Remember, God oversees their breakthroughs."

She slid her arms around his waist and hugged him. "You're right. I'm imagining the tension among the guests. Except Phil and Kris. That's real. Everyone else is a stranger to each other. People act different when they don't know each other." She moved away. "I'm following the cinnamon smell."

She left the room dressed in her sneakers, jeans, and a navy t-shirt. Comfort meant more to her than style, although she knew she looked fine and fit in with most of the guests' dress code.

Quiet reigned as she walked down the hallway to the kitchen, where Willow worked on breakfast. Her long blonde hair was wrapped in a messy chic bun at the nape of her neck, and choppy bangs hung halfway down her forehead.

"Good morning," Courtney said.

Willow jumped and put a hand to her heart. "Good thing I'm a young woman instead of an old lady, or I'd have dropped from fright."

"You're immersed in whatever you're stirring in that pot."

"I'm making a coating to dip toast in for tomorrow. I'm trying to prepare what I can ahead of time and see how it works."

"Yum, French toast! Too bad I have to wait until tomorrow. It's my favorite breakfast."

"You'll have to make do with my cinnamon rolls today." With her back turned to Courtney, a snicker punctuated the end of Willow's comment.

Her hands unclenched at the joking tone. A happy person. "Right. I'll leave you to it."

Courtney wandered into the great room to be greeted by the smell of coffee. Willow had placed a couple of carafes and a plate of cinnamon rolls on the roll-in cart. Courtney poured a cup of coffee and plated a roll. After grabbing a fork and a napkin, she sat at the head of the table.

At the sound of a door opening, she glanced up as Lauren entered from the hall where the guests' rooms were located. "Good morning," Courtney greeted her.

"Hi." Lauren appeared wide-awake. "I didn't realize anyone would be an early riser like me."

"I love the start of a brand-new day. Do you write this early in the morning?" She turned sideways to talk to Lauren, who stood at the food cart.

"I try to write before the rest of the world stirs." Lauren helped herself to a glass of water from the pitcher and eyed the cinnamon rolls.

"They don't bite," Courtney said.

"They look yummy."

Alex and Kris came into the room as Lauren took a seat with her own cinnamon roll, having decided not to pass them up.

"Good morning," Courtney greeted them.

Kris mumbled a reply as she trudged into the room, her face drawn like she hadn't slept much. She'd combed her hair and put on a green plaid shirt like yesterday's pink plaid. She wore jeans again. Courtney left her alone to wake up.

After she told their guests there would be a group meeting at 10:00 a.m. and lunch right after at 11:30, she left Alex to host while she went to work in their office. By 9:00 a.m., she decided to tidy up her and Alex's apartment while she had a few minutes.

She plodded along the hall between the offices and the guests' rooms. Directly at the end of the hallway was a door to the enclosed sunroom. For the winter and cool spring, it was heated by a separate heating unit. During the summer, it could be turned into a screened-in sunroom leading to the deck. She sighed—the deck, yet to be built, that would offer a great view of the Badlands in the distance.

Another hallway crossed this one before the sunroom door, leading to the stairwell up to the second floor. The other end of the hallway had an elevator to get to the second floor.

Passing the enclosed sunroom on the way to the stairs, she keyed in the code. Once she entered the stairwell, she heard voices coming from the enclosed sunroom. Loud voices.

She stopped on the first step and listened. She could make out most of their words, and it wasn't good.

CHAPTER 5

Courtney stood in the stairwell, listening.

"The truth will come out soon. Everyone will know exactly what you are." The venom in a young woman's voice cut through the air. Courtney didn't recognize the voice.

"What is it you think everyone will know?" Phil asked. "I haven't done anything wrong."

"You've stolen thousands of dollars from unsuspecting investors. You've ruined lives with your 'proven' theories on investments," the woman spat.

He laughed, and Courtney winced. Talk about pouring gasoline on a fire. "You have some individual vendetta. Is this by any chance personal?"

"Remember Hank?" the voice came out with a poisonous twist.

There was a pause before Phil answered in a softer voice, "He was weak. I never thought he'd give up on life."

Courtney wanted to know more about this Hank.

"I see you remember. His death is your fault."

Jade or Melanie, Courtney decided. She should quit listening to the private conversation, but she convinced herself problems between guests fell under need-to-know. And the woman had accused Phil of embezzlement.

"I didn't have anything to do with his death."

"Of course you did! You took everything from him and left him broke. And not only broke financially. Broken in spirit. You may not have pulled the trigger, but your actions caused him to take his own life."

"He didn't have to kill himself." Phil's whiny voice grated on Courtney. "He could have recovered."

"Recovered with what? Do you think he could recoup all the savings you stole at the age of sixty? He only had five years of work left before he retired. You're insane. You took everything from him and his family." The scorn rang clear in her voice.

"What do you want?" he asked.

"I wanted to tell you face-to-face: there are going to be repercussions. Your wife isn't safe. Take her away. Crocus Hill Inn isn't the best place for her right now."

"What do you mean? Are you threatening my wife?"

"A life for a life. She must know what you've been up to all these years. Wives usually do." A bitter laugh.

Courtney suspected Jade was the woman speaking with Phil.

"She had nothing to do with any of this and never knew anything about my business," Phil said.

"That might not matter when I make a decision. I'd suggest you find a reason to send her home."

The piercing hatred in her voice made Courtney back up against the step. What should she do? One guest threatened another. The serious words brought her to her senses. Should she interrupt?

"Kris insisted on coming. I have no idea how to convince her to go home. Especially if I stay," he objected.

"Well, find a way. We're only here for a week. One day soon, you won't be around to protect her. You know, your life for Hank's life."

"Now you're going to kill *me*?" Phil asked. "And you've told me ahead of time? You're crazy. What makes you believe you can get away with it? I'll be informing the police about our conversation. If something happens to me, they'll know who to arrest!"

"No, they won't. Besides, you're not going to the police. Guys like you believe you can figure out a way to stop me on your own, so you can keep getting away with stealing people's money. If you tell them about our conversation, you can bet they're going to comb through your financial dealings. They're going to find a lot of irregularities without any problem at all."

Silence again.

Then Phil warned, "Maybe you're the one who should be careful. I wouldn't go around threatening people you don't know. You're not going to hurt anybody. And you're not taking my money. Besides, the police already have information."

"I know you, Phil. You won't go to the police. You'll find a way around my ultimatum—which is confess or die. If it were up to me, your death would be the ultimate victory. While deciding what to do, time is ticking. In a few days, one way or another, your life is going to change. It's all in memory of Hank."

The next laugh taunted him. "I do have a gun."

"Quit pointing that thing at me. You're not going to do anything here." Phil's voice rose an octave.

What?! Courtney's heart raced as she jumped up from the stair where she'd sat down and fumbled to open the stairwell door into the hall.

"I could kill you and be done with all this, but what fun would that be? I want you to suffer and wonder when I'm coming after you."

When Courtney reached the hallway by the enclosed sunroom, she couldn't hear them anymore. Was she too late? She hadn't heard a shot. With trembling hands, she yanked at the enclosed sunroom door handle, and Jade hurried out carrying a shoe box. Ignoring Courtney, she slipped into her room.

Next, Phil hurried into the hallway from the enclosed sunroom, his face red and sweaty, and went into his room. No doubt to hide and update Kris. Courtney had no idea what he'd do. Alex needed to know, and they should contact the police. Plus, she needed Jade's gun but wasn't about to ask for it without professional help. Jade seemed too unpredictable.

She texted Braden and asked him to join her outside Jade's room. When he arrived, she left him there, telling him if Jade came out of her room to have her wait in the great room until Courtney talked to her. If she carried a shoebox, he should grab the box, no questions asked. Explanations could come later.

CHAPTER 6

Alex held Courtney as she cried. "I couldn't believe what I heard."

Courtney reported the conversation to the sheriff's office, and they promised to send someone out to talk to Phil and Jade. They weren't sure how long it would take them, but they'd make it a priority. She waited impatiently for the police to arrive.

"It's okay. We'll figure something out." Alex rubbed her back, soothing her.

They were in their office—rest would have to wait. "I'm sorry I opened this stupid inn." Another tear trickled down her cheek.

"You're upset. This will pass, and everything will work out okay." He continued to rub her back. "Do we make her leave? That's our legal right. We watch Jade until the police come. Plus, we need to take the gun away from her before something happens. If she gives us the gun, she can stay. Maybe we can help her."

What did he mean? "Help her shoot Phil?"

"Of course not. These people came here for issues in their life. Let's see if she wants counseling or to deal with whatever happened between this Hank guy and Phil."

He was right, but she didn't want to… She stopped mid-thought. That was what this whole program encompassed. "One of us should replace Braden. I needed a moment after telling you what happened with Phil and Jade to get myself together. When Jade does come out of her room, why don't we ask Braden to keep track of her until the sheriff comes?"

"Good idea. I hate keeping him from the lawn and backyard work, but this is an emergency. I'll take Braden out to the backyard and update him. You want to take hallway duty? I'll be back as soon as I tell him what's going on." He gave her another hug and left the room.

At least the group would be together during the meeting and lunch—which didn't leave much time for Jade to do anything before law enforcement arrived.

***

From the dining room window, they saw the sheriff arrive as Alex and Courtney were about to begin the ten o'clock morning meeting. Courtney caught Phil's eyes on Jade, and Jade smirked and winked at him. The others simply sat back and watched.

Courtney and Alex excused themselves to their guests and stepped outside to greet Sheriff Warren. They'd met him when the renovation of the inn resulted in an eight-year-old mystery being solved. "Thank you for coming. I'm not sure what to do about our guests."

"Courtney. Alex." He shook hands with them. He was a man in his sixties with gray hair touched with a youthful brown. He looked like he kept in good physical shape. Behind him stood another man, who was in his thirties, bald, with a thin and wiry build. "You obviously remember Deputy Lachlan. With discussion of a weapon, I thought it would be best to have two of us here."

She nodded at the deputy. He'd actually sold them the house they'd turned into this inn. "Thanks for coming. We're glad you're the deputy they sent. It's nice to see you again, despite the circumstances."

"Did you want to speak to Phil Young or Jade Nelson first?" she asked the sheriff.

"Let's talk to Mr. Young and then Ms. Nelson," he said.

As she led the sheriff through the great room, she asked Phil to join them. He didn't look surprised, but Kris did. While Courtney stood outside talking to the sheriff, Phil had a chance to decide on his story.

She led the sheriff, deputy, and Phil to the enclosed sunroom, which was at the end of the hallway where the guests' rooms were and where the threat took place. The sheriff allowed Courtney to stay, since she overheard the argument, but he told her not to interfere or speak unless spoken to during the interview.

After the sheriff sat across from Phil, the deputy pulled out his pencil and a small notebook. "Mr. Young, can you please describe to me what happened this morning?" the sheriff asked.

Phil faked confusion. "I'm not sure what you mean."

Courtney stared at him. *What?* She forced herself to keep her mouth shut.

The sheriff's face remained calm. "I mean when Jade Nelson threatened you with a gun." He kept his gaze steady.

"I have no idea what you're talking about." His voice came out with more force than necessary, and he frowned.

"A complaint filed with us identified you as being threatened with a weapon this morning. We take intimidation seriously." His calm gaze turned steely. "And we don't appreciate obstruction of justice. If someone threatened your life, we need to know."

"I have nothing to say." Glaring at the sheriff, Phil stood up and pushed his chair away, tipping it over. He left the chair on the floor and walked out of the enclosed sunroom.

"So much for his cooperation. Can you ask Ms. Nelson to come in the room?" the sheriff asked Courtney.

She stared at him as she stood. "Can you do anything if Phil doesn't cooperate?"

"We'll see what Ms. Nelson has to say." His steely expression remained in place.

Definitely getting the message the sheriff had finished sharing information, she went to find Jade. How would this conversation progress?

Jade waited in the great room with the others at the dining table as Alex continued with the ten o'clock meeting. Courtney gestured to Jade, who had already stood up, and led her back to the sunroom in silence.

The sheriff motioned Jade to sit across from him. The chair had been righted, and she sat down where Phil had his tantrum. Courtney resumed her earlier seat.

Staring at Jade, he waited for her to speak. Her expression remained serene as she took her time.

"What do you want to talk to me about?" Jade finally asked.

"This morning."

She tossed her black hair back, a pink strand flying loose. "What about this morning?"

"The gun. I'm talking about the gun you pointed at Mr. Young." He smiled at her when she jerked back in her chair.

Courtney hid her own shock. No lead-in questions, straight to the point. She admired the sheriff's technique.

"What gun?" she murmured as she looked down at the table.

Courtney almost groaned. If both people involved refused to speak, would the sheriff do anything about the threat against Phil? A gun was involved.

"Is that your final word?" he asked. "Are you sure you don't want to confess to what Mr. Young told us?"

Jade's expression turned mulish. "Phil did not say I threatened him with a gun, because I didn't. If he did, he's lying."

Courtney almost expected Jade to storm out of the room like Phil, but she didn't. She sat there and stared defiantly at the sheriff.

"We have your statement," he said, no expression on his face. "You can go."

Jade stared at him in surprise until it finally sank in he had finished questioning her. She hurried out the door.

Once the door closed behind Jade, Courtney turned to the sheriff. "What are you going to do? Can you search her room? I don't want any guns on this property." She stood up. "Let's go look for the gun."

He remained seated, although Gary stood. "I can't. Phil said she didn't do anything. Without his accusation, there's no crime."

Before the objection escaped her mouth, he held up his hand. "I know what you heard, and I believe you, but, legally, Phil needs to make the complaint. For some reason, he won't admit what happened."

Frowning, she huffed out, "Because she accused him of embezzlement, and that allegation would cause him a ton of problems."

The sheriff stood, and Gary pocketed his pencil and notebook. "I'm sorry. I'll check if Jade or Phil have been in trouble with the law in the past. Maybe something will come to light, especially if there is some embezzling scheme going on."

She nodded. "I understand what you're saying about not searching here, even though I don't like it. We'll probably tell Jade to leave, as guns aren't allowed on the premises."

"Be careful," the sheriff warned. "They had no compunction about lying. I believe you heard what you reported, but they refused to admit it. Don't put yourself in danger."

She nodded, not necessarily agreeing. A lot of thoughts ran through her head about Jade and Phil, prior relationships, and who Phil hurt, making Jade so angry.

The thought of having a potential murderer under her roof didn't sit well with Courtney. She tried one more desperate plea. "Can't you take her into custody while you check her background?"

He shook his head, real regret on his face. "I'm sorry."

"Okay." She'd wanted the police to take care of the problem, but she and Alex would have to ask Jade to give them the gun until she checked out of her room. Or she would have to leave the premises. The clock above the door showed it was a little after 11:00 a.m.

Courtney turned to face them, her hand on the knob of the door into the hallway. "Your vehicle is right in front of the window where they're all eating."

He laughed briefly and continued grinning at her mischievously. "Perfect. We'll walk right past, sending a message by the stern expression on our faces as we glare at them."

She laughed, appreciating that he'd let her see his more human side. "Good point. Thank you for coming out quickly. Maybe being warned the police know will stop Jade from doing anything before she leaves."

She let the sheriff and deputy take the lead down the hallway. As she waited for him to open the front door, she finally turned to all the watching guests. She caught Alex's gaze as he motioned toward the empty chair beside him with a slight nod.

She nodded and stepped outside with the sheriff and deputy.

"Remember what I said. Don't endanger yourself." The sheriff gave her a warning look as he got into the police vehicle.

Gary stopped by her side before he got into the sheriff's car. "You know where I am. I owe you and Alex a big favor, so call if you have a problem."

"I appreciate that." She hugged him. She could imagine Sheriff Warren's raised eyebrows, but he knew Gary was friends with her and Alex.

"Keep me updated." He got into the passenger seat, and she waved at them.

When she went back inside, she ignored everyone's stares and grabbed a small portion of food. After her stressful morning, her hunger was at a low ebb. She sat down next to Alex, relieved to see the guests looked relaxed. But what would happen next? They needed to do something proactive about Jade and her gun.

CHAPTER 7

Courtney watched Phil during the group's lunch. What had he told Kris about Jade's threats and the police visit?

As usual, Willow made a wonderful meal of lasagna and salad with garlic breadsticks. Phil played with his meal. He'd take a few bites and then push the rest to the other side of his plate.

His biting comments directed at Kris were subdued and rare. His wife looked at him as if she'd never seen this side of him. Phil didn't appear aware of her glances.

The rest of the table tried to act normal, as if the police hadn't questioned two of the guests. Lauren relayed a funny story about one of her readers. A reader who saw Lauren sitting behind a table with her books spread in front of her had asked when the author would arrive.

Lauren told the reader she was the author, at which point, the reader insisted she couldn't be. The author had to be much older, because the descriptions were insightful. Lauren told her about the research she'd done so older characters were portrayed correctly, which finally convinced the woman. There was no malice in her voice, and the reader seemed as amused as Lauren about the encounter.

"Ugh. Research." Melanie shook her head. "Not my forte. I always hated doing those papers in high school and college. I barely got through classes requiring essays. I can answer multiple choice questions easily, but my mind does not come up with full sentences when it's forced."

"What do you do for work?" Lauren asked her.

"I'm an accountant." The reddish highlights in her dark hair glinted in the sunlight coming from the big window by the table.

Phil's head lifted.

"You must have finished tax season," Lauren commented as she poured herself a glass of water from the carafe on the table in front of her.

"Yes, the ones needing filed by the fifteenth. Unfortunately, there's lots of clean up to go back to. People who filed extensions, and I'm sure all sorts of boring things the rest of you don't want to hear." She smiled. "I needed to take a break, although I miss my daughter."

"What's her name?" Lauren asked.

The whole table listened to their conversation as they finished their meal.

"Sylvia. She's ten." A brief frown crossed her face. "She wasn't happy her mother left for a week. She wanted to come with me."

"But you needed the break," Kris finally broke her silence. "We have two boys in good jobs. Well, they're grown up, but I remember trying to work extra hours and run the household. It takes a toll."

"It sure does," agreed Skylar, who'd joined them for lunch after she finished cleaning and straightening the rooms. "I have two little ones. A two-year-old and a four-year-old. I don't think I've slept for four years."

Courtney appreciated Skylar's help with cleaning and various duties at the inn. Skylar's mother, Lucy, took care of the kids while Skylar worked. So far, everything seemed to be going smoothly.

They all laughed, except Phil, who returned to staring at his plate. He'd somehow managed to eat all his food.

Courtney stood up and started clearing the plates. "Does anyone want dessert? It's apple pie with ice cream."

Jade, Skylar, Phil, and Kris refused, saying they couldn't eat another bite, and excused themselves from the table. Braden came into the house as the other diners left. He went over to the steel cart and filled his plate.

Courtney and Willow loaded another cart with dishes. "Willow has pie in the kitchen when you're ready," she said to Braden.

"Great." He took a giant mouthful, but ate neatly and quickly, like he always did. Courtney saw Alex hurrying too.

"How's it going in the garden area?" she asked Braden.

"I managed to till a nice row far enough from the house to do one row of grass with the lawnmower between the house and the flower bed. We'll get some good fertilized soil next week from

Ferguson's Feed. They have beautiful plants there. When it warms up in May, I'll take you there to pick out what flowers you want planted. In the fall, we'll plant bulbs for crocuses, tulips, and daffodils that will bloom next spring."

"Great." A feeling of warmth spread through her limbs at Braden's enthusiasm. When Alex suggested Braden needed somewhere to go for a while, she hesitated to hire him, but it was working out great.

Braden's suntan took away his sickly look, and his eyes weren't as haunted. Moments of mirth filled them at times. He deserved a break and to relax.

She and Alex refused dessert. Her time with the sheriff took away her appetite, and she wanted to discuss the situation with Alex alone. When she looked up from the table, she saw Skylar and Jade coming out of Jade's room.

She jumped up from her chair and grabbed Alex's sleeve. He followed her without question as she went to intercept the two women. She'd caught a glimpse of a box, which looked like the one Jade had with her earlier when she exited the sunroom. Skylar now carried it.

"Hey, Skylar," she called as she practically ran over to them. "Wait. I have a question."
As soon as she reached them, she snatched the box out of Skylar's hands. Since she surprised the younger woman, there was no resistance. Lifting the lid, she peeked into the shoebox. A hint of metal peeked out beneath a t-shirt. She moved the shirt aside and saw a gun.

She showed Alex, who stood beside her. "Let's go to the sunroom." Courtney bit her tongue to keep from screaming at Jade and Skylar as they all walked down the hallway. Anger coursed through her to the point she felt her head would explode.

Jade and Skylar followed silently. They sat down at the table closest to the door, and Courtney set the shoebox on the floor beside her chair. "I'm keeping the gun locked up until you leave, Jade. Alex and I will discuss when that will occur and let you know.

"You lied to the police this morning. I heard, and you know it. Obviously, you and Phil had dealings in the past, and we'll talk later." She looked at Skylar. "I want to know how you're involved?"

The two women exchanged glances, and Jade nodded at Skylar to answer.

"We're something like cousins." Skylar dropped her gaze before lifting it again to speak.

Courtney practically rolled her eyes. Was "like" a slang term? "What do you mean 'something like'?"

"Well, we aren't really cousins, but our families know each other. We have relatives in common, but my branch of the tree isn't the same branch as Jade's branch. However, we lived in the same community for a long time and are about the same age. We naturally became friends."

It dawned on Courtney. Skylar hadn't mentioned a connection before Jade arrived. "Why didn't you tell me you knew Jade?"

Skylar dodged the question. "It's only Monday. I wasn't here yesterday. I'm not sure when I would have told you."

Courtney clenched her jaws at the evasion, but the whole situation was wearing on her nerves. She needed a break. She glanced at Alex, who studied the women. Perhaps sensing her gaze, he looked at Courtney, a question in his eyes. She nodded.

"Skylar," he asked, "what were you going to do with the gun?"

"Take it home and hide it," Skylar admitted.

"And give it back when Jade asks for it?" Alex continued.

"Yes. Look, I don't know what's going on. Jade asked me to take it home until she was ready to leave. She told me she got in trouble having a weapon here and asked if I could keep it."

Courtney didn't know if she could believe anything anyone said at this point. "Why don't you assist Willow with lunch clean-up? We'll talk later."

Not wasting any time, Skylar hurried from the room. Jade watched her go and waited for them to speak.

Another look passed between Alex and Courtney. What were they going to do about Jade? They were adept at sensing each other's feelings.

"Jade, we can ban you from the inn due to the gun. Courtney and I are going to discuss what to do, and we'll let you know. You can go back to your own room or wander around. You have an appointment with Clarissa, our psychologist, this afternoon. I'd like you to keep that meeting."

Since they'd entered the enclosed sunroom, she hadn't said a word. She shrugged and left the room. All the bravado was gone, but Courtney sensed a hint of defiance.

Courtney looked at Alex. "We can kick her out for having a weapon on the premises."

"We could. But then she gets her weapon back and can stay in the area anyway."

They sat quietly. Courtney didn't know what to do. Alex was right. Or did they have to give the gun back? "Can we tell her to leave without returning it?"

"Maybe. I'll check with Nathan."

Having a lawyer for a brother came in handy. Would Jade hunt Phil and Kris down without a gun? Assuming she hadn't stashed another one somewhere.

Courtney could have used Clarissa's input as a psychologist, but she and Hugh hadn't returned from Bismarck yet.

She sighed. With Phil refusing to press charges against Jade, and she and Alex keeping the gun, she decided not to ask Jade to leave. Why was she so reluctant to do that? Because she understood Jade's anger over Phil embezzling money—if what she said was true.

CHAPTER 8

"Phil and Kris left for a drive in the country while we talked to Skylar and Jade," Courtney told Alex. "They plan to meet Rory and Ivy at the gun range and shoot for a while. Who wouldn't want to practice shooting after being threatened with a gun?"

They sat in their desk chairs, facing each other. Both of their desks were side by side in front of a large picture window overlooking the driveway and parking lot. Most of the spaces were empty because many of their guests were touring the countryside.

"I hope it's not to retaliate against Jade, but at least they left. Phil was silent at lunch and didn't so much as glance at Jade. He didn't snipe at Kris. Do you think he stole money from this Hank person Jade mentioned?" Alex straightened a stack of papers on his desk.

"Probably. He's a nasty man who ogled Jade. Or did—until today at lunch. Kris kept looking at him without him noticing. She knows there's something wrong."

Rolling his chair over to hers, he took hold of her hand. "I'm sorry this week started out on this note. We'll take care of Jade, and things will be smoother. I'm a big fan of this dream of yours and will do everything to help you make it work.

Despite Jade's vendetta against Phil. At least we're aware now."

Courtney's shoulders relaxed. She'd felt solely responsible for everything because the inn was her idea. She should have talked to Alex sooner. He would have supported her right away or at least listened, which would have cut down on her fear of failing. "Thanks. I appreciate it."

"As far as Phil goes, let's see what happens when he and Kris get back from their drive. They'll be seeing Clarissa this afternoon. Did Jade look upset when he flirted with her last evening?"

"No, she ate it up. Probably setting him up so he wouldn't suspect anything when she wanted to meet him this morning. They ignored each other in between police interviews. She didn't seem to care. She said what she wanted to say to him in the sunroom when she threatened him.

"She talked with Lauren and Melanie during lunch as if nothing happened. I think they all knew each other before they came here. I think they're already friends." Courtney played with the wedding ring on Alex's finger.

"But why would they keep it a secret? Must be the vacation-type relaxation making them friendly with each other. They don't have many options out here. Besides, so what if they're friends? Does it matter?"

"No. But it's odd if they are keeping it secret."

"Try not to worry about it. Remember, we set this place up so people who have problems can come and relax for a week, try to make decisions and get their heads together. Maybe those young ladies need to fix their relationship and didn't admit it on the form they filled out. Maybe they thought they could only mention one issue. Obviously, Phil has his issues, and he's here, isn't he?" Alex asked.

"Possibly. But when they arrived, remember how Phil complained about coming here, and Kris reminded him it was his choice?"

"Yes, but Kris knows they have problems, and here they are." He got up from his chair and coaxed her to her feet.

When she stood, he put his arms around her and gave her a warm hug. "It's going to work out."

The warmth of his body seeped into hers. He was right. God was in charge.

He squeezed her shoulder lightly. "Right. Let's finish this up. Clarissa did agree to all the appointments, didn't she?"

"Yes. She's looking forward to counseling them as much as she can in a week."

"Maybe she and Hugh will decide to move to Elm City permanently. You'll be better once we get through this first group of guests. Let's focus on the sense of accomplishment you'll have when some of these people leave feeling like they've restarted their lives."

Courtney laughed. "Just some of them?"

"Well, we can expect miracles, but not everyone's going to solve their problems in a week."

"No. No, they won't." Her mind returned to Phil. Phil and Kris better leave alive, even if they didn't make any progress from the week's program.

She felt uneasy after the Phil and Jade fiasco, but
there were no guarantees in life. She braced herself
for the rest of the week.

CHAPTER 9

Melanie, Lauren, and Jade returned from exploring the countryside first. Melanie went out with Jade, but her appointment with Clarissa limited their outing to only a half hour. Lauren drove by herself but wasn't gone long either.

Courtney led Melanie to the last door at the end of the hallway, where Clarissa's office was located next to Alex and Courtney's. She knocked on the closed door.

"Come in."

At the sound of Clarissa's invitation, Courtney opened the door and motioned Melanie forward. "I'd like to introduce you to Dr. Clarissa Alois. She used to be a psychologist in a Bismarck hospital but moved here to treat patients in the area. Dr. Alois, this is Melanie Percel."

Clarissa got up from where she sat behind her desk and came around to shake hands with Melanie. "You can call me Clarissa." Her dark brown eyes held a welcome that warmed Courtney the first time she'd met her at the hospital where she worked before joining them at the inn. They'd met through Alex's brother, Paul, who also worked at the hospital.

Melanie must have felt the warmth of her smile too, because she let out a breath and said a quiet thank you.

"Melanie, you can have a seat there." She pointed to a dark blue armchair in front of her cherry-wood desk. "We're going to visit for a while. Everything you say will stay between us."

She turned to Courtney. "Thank you."

Courtney closed the door behind her when she left.

***

Courtney found Jade and Lauren in the television room, watching a movie. They were both laughing and enjoying popcorn and candy. They told her they were waiting for their appointments with Dr. Alois. She left them to it.

She noted Kris and Phil's vehicle was still gone.

Braden worked in the backyard, and Skylar left for the day. Willow was preparing the evening meal in the kitchen.

Which left Rory and Ivy. She spent the least amount of time with them. How were they getting along? Their vehicle was gone from the parking lot, so they must have been out touring the area or with Phil and Kris at the gun range. If she had been able to attend the morning meeting, she might have known more about them. Unfortunately, the police visit curtailed her participation.

The guests had plenty of sightseeing to do when they weren't at the inn. The city of Medora was about twenty miles away and catered to tourists, although this early in the year, not everything would be open. Elm City was small and didn't have much going on. The country lanes were beautiful, the Badlands shining dark blue and gray in the background with their valleys and hills. They were a majestic sight.

Alex joined her in the great room at the kitchen table. "Anything happening?"

"Nope. Television for Lauren and Jade, Melanie's talking to Clarissa, and the rest are off doing their own thing." She stretched out her legs. "I'm thinking of checking out Braden's progress in the backyard."

"Let's go."

CHAPTER 10
Monday Afternoon

As they entered the house after talking to Braden in the backyard, Courtney's cell phone rang. She pulled it out and glanced at the call screen but didn't recognize the number. "Hello. Courtney Richmond of the Crocus Hill Inn."

"Oh, Courtney. This is Kris." The voice on the other end of the line ended with a sob. "I'm glad I reached you. Patty from the diner gave me your number. I should have programmed it into my cell phone but didn't think of it."

She spoke fast and gasped for air. Courtney concentrated on getting the gist of the words. "What's wrong, Kris?"

"I can't find Phil. He never came back for me." Kris sobbed hysterically.

"Are you with Patty?" Courtney asked. Poor Kris. After this morning's threat from Jade, she must be terrified. Had Jade done something to Phil? Her heart sank at the thought.

"Yes. I'm at her diner. Johnny's in the kitchen."

"Can you hand her the phone?" Maybe Patty could give her a coherent account.

"Hi." Patty's calm voice soothed her ear.

"Hi. Thanks for taking care of Kris. What's going on?" Courtney had gotten to know Patty and her husband Johnny in the past eight months.

"Her husband, Phil, left her in Elm City to wander around and view the town. They'd been out driving and went to the shooting range south of town for a while. Kris said their fellow guests Rory and Ivy mentioned stopping there. Kris wasn't having a good time, so Phil brought her into town and left her at my diner. He went back out to the shooting range."

"That all sounds okay." Courtney didn't hear anything concerning, except her gut argued something was wrong. Patty wouldn't have told Kris to call her if everything was okay.

"Phil didn't come at three o'clock to pick her up as arranged. Kris left the café after she sat in the diner for a while visiting. She left to wander around town and look at people's flowers and houses.

"She stopped at a few of the other shops in town. When her husband didn't show up at three o'clock as planned, she wandered up and down the streets, thinking maybe she'd missed him somewhere. When she couldn't find him, she came back to the diner, and here we are. It's four o'clock, and you know I would have seen their vehicle arrive in town with my view. He's only an hour late, but she said it's not like him."

"It's not," Kris called from the background. "He's always on time."

"Maybe he and Rory and Ivy went somewhere else together," Courtney suggested.

Again, her fear Jade followed through on her threat sent a shiver of dread down her spine.

"I told her, but my biggest concern is he isn't answering her calls or texts. She wants to call the sheriff, but I don't believe he'll be too worried when Phil's only an hour late," Patty said.

But Patty didn't know about Jade's threats to Phil. Courtney's heart rate amped up, but she tried to stay calm.

"He would answer my calls if he could. I know there's something wrong," Kris said, her voice stronger. A slight vibration remained to remind Courtney of her tears.

Courtney spoke to Patty again. "Thanks for not putting us on speaker, so she can only hear your side. I'm going to send Braden into town to pick up Kris and bring her back to the inn. I'll tell her in a minute when you give her phone back to her. But I'm concerned too. If Phil hasn't been answering, there probably is something wrong. I'm going to call Rory and Ivy to see if they're with him."

And then she would call the sheriff and report Phil missing. Maybe they'd ordinarily wait longer to check out a missing person, but not after this morning's threat.

"A good plan," Patty agreed.

"Braden should be there in about ten minutes. Thanks, Patty. Can you give the phone back to Kris?" Courtney had been so involved in the conversation, she'd forgotten Alex was in the room listening. Braden must have gone to get some more food from Willow.

Courtney muted her phone for a second before Kris got back on the line. "Alex, can you tell Braden I need him to run into town?"

He nodded and strode away.

Kris came back on the phone. "What are we going to do? Patty said the sheriff won't get involved because it's only been a short time. It seems like hours to me," she said in an angsty tone.

"Don't worry. I'll get the sherif involved." He would certainly come to the inn now Phil was missing, since Jade threatened him and Kris earlier that morning. "Maybe it's some mix-up, but we'll have the police check it out anyway. Braden is going to pick you up and bring you back here, and—"

"But how will Phil find me if I'm not here?" Her voice faltered as she wept.

Courtney hoped Kris could hold herself together until they found Phil. She didn't know what she'd do if someone threatened Alex, and he was missing. "Text Phil you'll be at the inn. I'm going to call Rory and Ivy. You don't have their numbers, do you?"

"No. We never exchanged them." She sniffled.

"Okay. Let me call them to see what they know. Patty will keep an eye out for your husband and let him know what's going on if he comes back to Elm City. Maybe he missed your text because of phone problems. When he doesn't find you there, he'll borrow a phone or return to the inn. Most likely his phone ran out of charge, or he's in a zone without coverage." Courtney hoped that was the case.

"Okay…" She sighed heavily, weariness evident in her voice.

"We'll find him," Courtney reassured her. "If Rory and Ivy don't know anything about Phil's whereabouts, the sheriff's deputies will be on the lookout for him in case his vehicle broke down somewhere along the road."

"Thank you." A smidgen more liveliness lifted her voice.

"Braden should be there in about ten minutes to get you. I'm calling Rory and Ivy now." She hung up. Turning to Alex and Braden, she asked, "Did you get to eat?"

Braden held his vehicle keys in one hand and a water bottle in the other. He'd changed into clean clothes. "Sure. I ate as soon as I got to the kitchen."

Remembering how fast he could eat reassured Courtney. "Phil left Kris to wander around Elm City while he went back to the gun range to practice with Rory and Ivy. He planned to be back an hour ago to pick her up. He hasn't shown up and isn't answering his phone."

"Not good. The not answering his phone part," Braden said. "Although he could be in a zone with no cell coverage."

"Agreed. Anyway, Kris is at Patty's Diner. Can you pick her up and bring her back here?"

"Sure. I'm on my way. I'll keep an eye out for their vehicle in case something happened to it on the road. I remember what it looks like."

Ah, yes. Braden liked vehicles of all kinds. "Thanks, Braden."

When he left, Courtney went over to Alex and leaned against him. He put his arms around her in a tight hug. "It's going to be okay," he said against her hair.

"I know. I needed a moment to get it together. Kris was hysterical. You know Jade was gone earlier, and Phil is missing. My imagination is conjuring bad scenarios. Could Jade have done something?"

"We'll find him."

She pulled away, taking a step back. "I'm trying to convince myself you're right. With Jade's threats this morning, it's hard to do."

"I know, I'd like to promise you everything is okay. But, honestly, I'm feeling the same fear you are." He took her hands in his. "Whatever's going on, we'll figure it out." He squeezed her hand in sympathy.

"Well, I better check with Rory and Ivy." How she wanted them to say they knew where Phil went, and he wasn't missing. Her clammy hands didn't agree with that thought.

Alex followed her to their office, standing beside her as she sat in her desk chair, searching her desk for the guests' cell phone numbers. She dialed Rory first.

He answered at once. "Hi. This is Rory."

"Hi, Rory. This is Courtney from Crocus Hill Inn. I'm sorry to interrupt your afternoon, but is Phil with you, by any chance?"

"No. He left about two thirty. He needed to get back to Elm City to pick up Kris. We were at the gun range, then Ivy and I went on a back road tour," he said.

Courtney heard Ivy giggle in the background and wondered if there had been a make-out session on the tour, but she didn't care. She had her answer. "Okay. Thanks. We'll see you when we see you. Have fun."

"We will." He hung up.

She stared at Alex. "They haven't seen Phil since two thirty when he left them at the gun range, so he could pick up Kris. I'm going to have to notify the sheriff's department. We can't ignore Jade's threat with Phil missing. What do you think?"

"Good idea. I'm going out to the gun range. They're open until seven since there are more daylight hours. There's no sense in calling over there. If he left, the staff won't know any more than Rory and Ivy. I'll drive a few different routes around there, seeing what I can find." Alex pulled his keys out of his pocket.

"Sure. Why don't you call me every half hour if you can?" Courtney needed him to stay in touch.

He raised his eyebrows. "Are you worried about me?"

"Don't sound surprised. I hate to burst your bubble, but I'm more concerned about keeping Kris in the loop, or I get the feeling she's going to fall apart." She could tell he knew the truth.

He hugged her. "I know you're worried about me too."

"Of course." She gave him a quick peck on his lips. "Get going, so Kris knows we're trying to do something. I'll call the sheriff and remind him of this morning's events. His deputies can be on the lookout for any stranded vehicle. Again, I don't know what else to do to appease Kris. I don't know enough about Phil to know whether to be worried about him or not."

"There's one thing I know. Their vehicle has North Dakota plates, but they said they were from Montana. Don't know why." Alex shared the information casually, although his tone showed tension.

"Why didn't you tell me before?" Courtney tried to hide her irritation. There had been no reason earlier for her to care about that information.

"I didn't want to worry you. They might have a simple reason for having a North Dakota vehicle."

"You're right." She tried to relax her shoulders. "I'm upset about this whole situation. We don't need to start out with a guest getting lost." She didn't add, "or murdered."

"Don't worry. He's a grown man." He gave her one more hug. "Why don't you see if Gary's working today? If he's not on deputy duty, he can look around back roads. I'll be in touch."

"Thanks." She knew he kept things low-key to comfort her, but she'd seen the concern in his eyes. The implication of Phil missing after this morning's threats from Jade upset him too.

She called the sheriff's office and was connected to the sheriff himself. She gave her name, explaining Phil appeared to be missing.

"Phil was the person threatened this morning, right?" Sheriff Warren asked.

"Yes. His wife says it's out of character for him not to pick her up at the time they planned. She said he's reliable. They're not from around here, so I suggested he could be lost and out of cell range."

The sheriff agreed he'd notify his deputies, and they'd start searching. He asked for the license plate number. Fortunately, Courtney asked Alex for the information before he left, and he'd given her the North Dakota plate number.

"If you need to talk to the wife, she will be back soon. One of our staff went to pick her up from Elm City," Courtney informed him.

"Okay. We'll do some looking around. Do you know who saw him last and where?" the sheriff asked.

"He left Kris in Elm City to sightsee and went to the gun range to practice shooting with another couple who are guests here, Rory and Ivy. He was supposed to return to Elm City at three to pick up Kris.

"I called Rory," Courtney told him. "He said Phil left on time to pick up his wife. That's the last time anyone saw him. Alex went over to the rifle range to drive around the area in case Phil had car trouble."

"Okay. I'll let you know if we find anything." He sounded concerned and in a hurry, which raised her blood pressure and intensified her fears.

"If he returns here, we'll let you know right away." Courtney hung up and called Gary, who answered after the first ring. "I need a favor."

"Sure. That was quick," he said, his voice teasing.

"It's about this morning and that gun situation."

"Oh no." All levity disappeared from his voice.

"Phil's missing. He hasn't been seen since around 2:30 p.m. Are you working?" she asked.

"Yes."

"You'll probably hear from the sheriff soon about keeping an eye out for Phil's vehicle." She gave him the license plate.

"It's going to be okay, Courtney. Pray."

She smiled at that. She'd been working with Gary to believe in God, and now Gary was reminding her. "Right." She hung up. She'd done all she could except pray, which she began doing immediately.

She went to see what the other guests were doing and to make up a tray with tea and coffee for Kris when she got back. Although, having been at Patty's, she'd probably already had plenty of beverages.

Melanie and Jade had finished their appointments with Clarissa and were reading books in the nooks of the room. Lauren wasn't around. Courtney assumed she was writing in her room or with Clarissa.

Courtney would have to look at the schedule on the bulletin board for appointment times. Obviously Kris and Phil missed their appointment, as had Rory and Ivy. She'd have to stress to them all that meeting with Clarissa was part of the program.

She got a text from Alex.

Just arrived at gun range. Going in now.

Thanks, she texted back.

CHAPTER 11

Courtney heard Clarissa and Hugh talking in the hallway. Soon they joined Courtney by the kitchenette island.

"How are things going?" Clarissa asked. "I was busy writing some patient notes in my office when I heard lots of activity in the hallway."

"We have a situation but hope it's a crossing of wires, and nothing's wrong. One of the guests is missing." Aware Jade and Melanie could hear every word, she decided it didn't matter. They would know as soon as Kris returned.

So far, she and Alex hadn't revisited the situation with Jade as they waited for Courtney's brother to get back to them on whether to make her leave the inn. He was probably in court, or he would have called her.

"I'm assuming it's one of the couples, because everyone else showed up for their appointment." Clarissa brought her back to the moment.

"You're right. Phil drove Kris to Elm City and went back to the gun range alone to meet Rory and Ivy. He hasn't reappeared to pick up Kris. She's waiting at Patty's Diner for Braden to pick her up." Courtney watched Jade's puzzled expression. It seemed genuine.

Clarissa settled at the dining table. Hugh sat beside her.

"It could be a mix-up." Courtney felt repeating the phrase would make it true.

Clarissa tapped the table with her finger. "You're probably right."

Courtney plopped into a chair beside them, slumping in her seat. She'd filled Clarissa and Hugh in on the situation between Jade and Phil before Clarissa started seeing everyone. She glanced at Jade and Melanie, listening avidly to the conversation, no longer pretending to read.

Clarissa stopped tapping her finger on the table. "I'll wait for Kris and let you know as soon as she returns. Why don't you and Hugh go to your office to wait?"

Courtney happily left the room, appreciating Clarissa's suggestion.

Jade and Melanie stood and joined Clarissa. Neither said anything until Hugh and Courtney left the room. As they walked down the hallway to Hugh's office, Courtney heard them asking Clarissa questions.

Once they closed the office door, Courtney looked at Hugh. They didn't even move away from the closed door.

"Thought you might want to say a quick prayer in private." Hugh guided her to an office chair. "You know, part of my spiritual calling at the inn as resident deacon."

She appreciated his light manner, a pleasant change from the day's drama. Her phone chirped with Alex's ringtone. "You pray. I'll answer this call."

"What's going on?" she asked Alex.

"I found him, Courtney." The somber tone made her sit straight up in her chair. "It's not good."

"Tell me." Her voice and hands shook.

"He's been shot. I found him lying on the road beside his vehicle. There's a gun on the ground beside him, and he's dead. I called the sheriff."

She caught a hint of a sob in her husband's voice and wished they were within touching distance. "I'm sorry you were the one to find him. Now we know what happened."

"Right. I'll have to wait for the sheriff's department to get here. Only tell Clarissa and Hugh. Let the police tell Kris."

"I don't want to leave her in the dark, but I guess it's for the best." The sheriff would want to break the news to Kris, but it made her uncomfortable to make her wait a moment longer than necessary. "The police won't want us to interfere, but it sounds like someone killed him." She couldn't say "murdered."

"Someone from the sheriff's office has arrived. I have to go. I love you," he said.

"Love you too."

Lost as to what to do, Courtney gazed around the room, then over at Hugh, who sat in Alex's desk chair. She floundered. "After Jade's threat this morning, I was afraid for Phil and Kris. Then we got the gun from Jade, and I convinced myself everything was okay. I messed up.

"If Jade did this… Alex found Phil lying on the ground by his vehicle. He was shot. Either she had another gun, or someone else killed him." She stumbled over her words, tears filling her eyes.

Hugh leaned over and patted her on the shoulder. "It's not your fault. It's the fault of whoever killed him. Let's say a prayer."

She slipped her phone back into her pocket and folded her hands in prayer.

"God, please be with Kris during this time of trial. Whatever Phil did on earth, please forgive his sins, and let him into Your light. Please help those of us near Kris assist her during the coming days in whatever way we can. Amen."

"Amen," Courtney echoed. "I guess we need to go back and keep this all to ourselves. You can tell Clarissa whenever you have a moment alone with her."

Hugh nodded. "I don't want to leave Kris in the dark, but no doubt Alex is right. That's a job for the police. You've worked with Sheriff Warren and Gary. You know what they want us to do better than me. I'll get Clarissa alone to tell her what happened to Phil."

Maybe Clarissa and Hugh would be useful to Kris—they both knew how to comfort and listen. They returned to the great room. Kris would arrive any second.

CHAPTER 12

Hugh and Courtney rejoined the others in the great room as Willow brought in the food. When Courtney asked if she wanted help, Willow declined. Courtney had lost track of time, not realizing the guests were probably hungry.

Kris would be back any minute with Braden, wanting to know if there was any news. Courtney didn't want to lie to her and hoped the sheriff would arrive soon. Her thoughts kept whirling from Kris to the guests sitting in the great room to the possibility Jade killed Phil.

As it happened, Braden returned with the sheriff's cruiser following him up the drive.

Courtney stood outside the front door waiting for them. Braden barely stopped the vehicle when Kris slid out of the passenger side.

"What's happening? What do you know?" Kris ran up the stairs and grabbed Courtney's arm.

Courtney, courage failing her, pointed to the sheriff's cruiser. "Let's see if they have news."

Kris vibrated with anxiety, shifting her weight from leg to leg as she waited for the sheriff and his deputy to get out of their vehicle. She ran back down the stairs to them. "Have you found Phil? Where is he?"

The sheriff took off his hat, twirling it slowly in his hands. He looked down at Kris, whose face showed recent tears. "Let's go inside to talk." Then he looked up at Courtney standing at the top of the steps.

When the others joined her inside the front door, Courtney introduced them. "This is Kris Young. Her husband, Phil, is missing. Kris, this is Sheriff Ray Warren and Deputy Gary Lachlan. We can talk in the sunroom alone." She indicated the other people in the room watching them.

Kris's energy waned, as if she knew something bad was coming. Her gait slowed.

"Thank you, Braden." He stood by the door watching them. "We'll handle this, but I'll call you if we need something."

He looked like he wanted to stay but turned and went back outside.

Courtney led the sheriff, Gary, and Kris past the other guests eating at the table. She mentally thanked whoever got the guests to the table quickly, keeping them occupied. She wished Alex had returned before the sheriff, but they might be asking him questions at the scene. At least Gary was the deputy who'd come with the sheriff, and since they were friends, she relaxed slightly.

At the end of the hallway, she opened the door, and they all filed into the sunroom.
Gary carried a laptop case. There were two tables, and the sheriff sat at the side of the one closest to the door. Seated at the other table, Gary pulled out his laptop and opened it. Courtney and Kris joined the sheriff.

Kris kept staring at him as they sat down. Her hands twisted together, never stopping. "I've been patient. Now tell me what's going on," she demanded, leaning toward the sheriff, wringing her hands. "Where is my husband?"

"I'm sorry to tell you he is dead, Mrs. Young," Sheriff Warren told her in a hushed, sympathetic voice.

Courtney reached over to cover Kris's hands. They stilled at Courtney's touch.

Kris slumped in her chair. Tears filled her eyes. "What happened? Did he have a heart attack? But he's only in his fifties. He's too young to have a heart attack. And where was he? Where did you find him?"

The sheriff waited patiently until Kris's questions came to a halt.

His glacial-blue eyes softened into a peaceful sky blue, although Courtney didn't doubt for a minute they watched every move she made. "Out on one of the country roads near the gun range. Someone called us, and we went out there to see what happened. He'd been shot."

Kris leapt up from her chair. "She did it. That hussy did it! I knew it. I told Phil to stay away from her, but what does he do? He sets up another time to meet her. Arrest her right now!" she demanded.

The sheriff looked past Courtney halfway through Kris's angry diatribe, and Courtney heard the scrape of a chair behind her. She turned around and saw Gary get to his feet. She moved her own chair so she could see the sheriff and the deputy at the same time.

"Don't move, ma'am. You want me to arrest her?" The sheriff calmly pointed at Courtney.

"Not her," Kris huffed. "I mean Jade. The woman who threatened Phil this morning. He said you talked to her."

"We're going to need more information from you before we arrest anyone. What do you mean, he met her again?"

"He saw her this morning. She'd left a threatening note under the door. It said if he didn't meet her, she'd tell everyone…" She closed her mouth and sat down, swallowing audibly. "Well, she threatened him."

"How did she threaten him?" the sheriff asked.

"She pulled out a gun and pointed it at him." Her voice faded away as she sagged in her chair.

"He denied the accusation this morning," the sheriff reminded her gently.

"He didn't want to cause problems for her. He said if he lied, she'd be okay. I told him he needed to take her threat seriously." She burst into tears.

The sheriff waited for her to get herself together again. "I need to see the note you found under the door." He motioned for the deputy to sit. Gary sat and resumed typing.

"Uh." Kris's hands twisted in and out of each other again. "We got rid of the note."

Sheriff Warren leaned back in his chair. "Why would you do that? If she threatened you, wouldn't you want to keep it to show someone? Either us or the police in Minot?"

"Minot? Here in North Dakota? Didn't Courtney tell you Phil and I are from Montana?" Her hands suddenly stilled. She glared at Courtney. "All our paperwork said we're from Montana. What's this about Minot?"

Courtney knew their car had a North Dakota license plate but nothing about a move from Minot, North Dakota, to Montana. The police must have found out a few things when they searched their database for Phil and Kris Young.

"We looked up his driver's license. The address on it was in Minot." Sheriff Warren moved forward. "Does that refresh your memory?"

"We moved recently." Kris looked down at her hands resting on the table.

"Really?"

"Why are you even asking me?" Kris stared at him now. "I told you about Jade threatening him."

"Where were you during the time he was killed?"

"Wandering around Elm City, or with Patty, waiting for him." Kris's glare had swiveled from Courtney to the sheriff.

"How do you know when he died?" Sheriff Warren's eyes turned back to glacial blue.

"During the time Phil dropped me off in Elm City until Braden came to pick me up, I was stuck in Elm City. I didn't have a vehicle. Elm City is small," she said contemptuously. "I'm sure if I'd gotten a ride somewhere, someone would have seen me. Now, what are you going to do about Jade?"

"Did she sign the note?"

"No. But she met him at the time the note specified and threatened him, so it must have been her." Kris's voice rose in frustration.

"Jade pointed a gun at Phil. Then what happened?" His eyes might have been glacial, but his soft voice coaxed a response. He knew when to bring it out.

Courtney admired his back-and-forth demeanor. Stern, then soft. Of course, he'd already heard from Courtney, Jade, and Phil about the morning's events.

"It doesn't matter. Phil's gone, and so is the note. Besides, Courtney overheard some of the conversation and told you." She collapsed against the back of her chair. Tears filled her eyes. "Jade killed Phil. You know it. I'm afraid of her. She arranged the meeting with him this morning, pointing a gun at him. Told him she would get him someday, leaving him there. She wanted him to wonder when she'd kill him. He told me all about it when he got back from talking to her. It didn't take long to follow through on her threat. I guess I'm next."

Sheriff Warren stood up, gesturing to the deputy. "Why don't we let Mrs. Young rest while we talk to Jade?"

"She's probably eating with the other guests." Courtney touched Kris on the arm. "Let's go to your room. You can tell me if you need anything. If not, I'll leave you to rest. I'm sure you don't want to go back to the group."

Kris shuddered. "No. I couldn't eat a bite or see anyone. I could use a cup of tea, though. It might settle my stomach."

She turned to the sheriff and deputy. "I'll send Jade back here."

Gary got up, following Kris and Courtney to the sunroom door. "I'll go get her."

"She's at the dining table, unless she left while we talked."

When they got to Kris's room, Courtney promised to bring her the tea. She suddenly remembered she'd forgotten to tell the sheriff about the gun she and Alex took from Jade right after lunch.

She left Kris, calling down the hallway, "Gary!"

He turned.

"Can you come back for a minute?" she asked. "It's important."

Gary turned around, rejoining her as she went back into the sunroom. She told them about seeing Skylar and Jade talking and the gun in the shoebox. She mentioned the gun was locked up in her and Alex's personal safe upstairs in their apartment.

The sheriff didn't look happy. "Thank you for the information. I wish you told me this as soon as you saw the gun."

She bit her lip. "I know. I'm sorry. Things were tense. Then Phil was missing, and I forgot."

"Well, it's done now. Deputy, can you go get Ms. Nelson now?"

The deputy left the room. After one more apology, Courtney went to get Kris her tea. She was relieved to see Alex sitting at the table with the guests. "What's going on?"

"Jade." Gary stood beside Courtney. "Do you have a minute?"

Jade got up slowly from the table. Quiet determination and an intelligent stare replaced her flirtatious manner. "I know what you're going to say, but I didn't do anything."

She stood in the middle of the great room and glanced back at the table. "One of them is responsible, but I don't know who."

"Let's talk about that." Gary stepped back a pace to let her go first.

Jade's willingness to accompany the deputy surprised Courtney, although Jade knew Courtney had the gun used to threaten Phil earlier in the day. She half expected Jade would disappear while they talked to Kris. But, instead, here she was willing to talk.

Alex stood up from the dining table in the great room and joined her at the end of the hallway where the guests couldn't hear. Rory and Ivy must have returned while she was in the other room, because all the guests sat at the table, along with Clarissa and Hugh.

"You might want to call Nathan," she told him.

He nodded.

The sheriff heard her request as he stood in the sunroom doorway. For some reason, Jade had halted in the middle of the great room.

"Alex isn't sharing anything with anybody." Sheriff Warren's chest was puffed out in the stance most law enforcement used when displaying their authority.

"Nathan's our lawyer and my brother. We need to know the legal ramifications of having a dead guest. That sounds cold, but our business depends on reputation." Courtney's words had no effect on the sheriff.

"Alex and Nathan won't spread the word to anyone else until you release the information. Alex and I have gone through a few things without an attorney, and I'm not willing to do that again. Aside from talking to Nathan, our guests' feelings come first, and we have the best professionals to help them."

The sheriff stood there for a minute. Even though he was a slender man, his height intimidated her, and the hallway walls closed in on her.

Finally, he nodded. "Fair enough, but no one else."

"We agree. And I speak for Alex. We don't want this getting out any more than you do. We opened this week. We can't afford bad publicity." Courtney knew how cold that sounded when a man lay dead.

"You know I shouldn't let you in on the interview with Jade." His face remained a still mask. She had no idea what he was thinking.

"Then why are you?" Her heart beat loudly in her ears.

"I have my reasons, and you heard her threats this morning. You can tell me if her responses match what you know. But," he raised a finger, "don't plan on being in on every interview."

She nodded. Maybe Jade would crumble, confess, and this would be over. Unfortunately, life didn't usually turn out easy. She'd know after the police interviewed Jade. Courtney looked down the hallway to see where she was.

Jade stopped at the threshold of the great room into the hallway, turning back to look at the guests, who all sat around the dining table. "I'm telling the police everything."

CHAPTER 13

Everyone froze at Jade's words, except Courtney and Alex, who rushed back to the great room. Something must have happened with Jade before the deputy came to get her. Now the police wanted to know why everyone was staring at her.

The deputy and sheriff joined everyone in the great room.

"I told you not to bring any weapons." Braden gazed around the table. "We agreed. No violence. Jade's threat to Phil this morning is all on her."

Alex caught Braden's attention, and their eyes met. Braden ducked his head but not before a flash of guilt crossed his face. Alex frowned.

Courtney's brow wrinkled. What was going on? Braden knew.

She didn't have a chance to ask because tires sounded on gravel outside. A Minot City Police car pulled into the staff parking lot outside the window where they all sat. Alex looked at Braden again.

Braden stared out the window, relaxing back into his chair. His face eased into a neutral expression.

The relief surprised Courtney, since Braden spent time in prison. She would have thought his stomach would be in knots, like her own, but he seemed not to feel the same way. This led to another thought: Braden might have been expecting them.

Alex walked over to Braden. "Do you know why they're here?"

"Yes." Guilt flashed across his face again. "I can explain."

"It might be too late, but when the police tell us what they want, and we have a minute, you can fill me in." Everyone stared at the front door as Alex opened it for the Minot Police. "I'm the inn co-owner, Alex Richmond."

He introduced the sheriff and deputy, who stepped closer to the door with Courtney, while Jade backed away. "Sheriff Warren and Deputy Lachlan from Elm County. I don't know if you've met them before?"

They shook hands with the sheriff and deputy, introducing themselves as Detective Zueger and Detective Entz to Alex and Courtney.

Detective Zueger took control. "Hi, Sheriff. It's been a while, except for our short conversation this afternoon. Deputy Lachlan, hello."

They returned greetings.

"I don't know how far you've gotten with the investigation, but I decided to come in person to fill you in on this group." Detective Zueger glanced at Braden. "We know a few of the guests this week, as I told you on the phone."

Legs shaking, Courtney sat down on the edge of the armchair nearest the front door. What was happening?

Alex glared at Braden, then Courtney noticed the detective's attention on Braden for a second. Braden knew what was going on but hadn't told her or Alex, or Alex wouldn't look so angry. She was angry too. And hurt.

The sheriff nodded. "We need to exchange information before we continue with interviews. How about we leave Deputy Lachlan and Detective Entz here with the guests? We can go out to the sunroom to discuss everything?"

"Sounds good," Detective Zueger said.

He followed the sheriff back down the hallway. Detective Entz and the deputy stood at the end of the hallway.

The sheriff stopped and turned around. "Someone brought a gun earlier, which has been confiscated, but, be aware, any one of the guests might be armed. Might want to keep an eye out." Then he continued back to the sunroom.

Why did the sheriff add the part about keeping an eye out? Like the gun would be on display. Alex saw the murder weapon on the ground where Phil was shot.

The deputy stood by the door to the outside, and the other detective stood over by the fireplace, covering the room. Jade returned to her place at the table.

Courtney wouldn't be allowed to hear their conversation in the sunroom, although she almost followed them out of the room to stand in the corner by the stairwell again. Unfortunately, it would be too obvious.

But she had Braden in her sights. "So, Braden, what's going on? We're stuck here for a while. Since the detective standing here already knows, you might as well tell us."

Braden pushed his plate away, leaning back in his chair. He swiped his hand through his black curly hair, which belied his relaxed posture. "Phillip Young was a crooked investment counselor who practiced in Minot. He had lots of victims, but no one could get the proof they needed to get him prosecuted. A bunch of us got together because our relatives suffered by being scammed, and we decided to find the proof."

"Why didn't you tell us?" Alex demanded as he stood a foot away, looking down at Braden. "We would have helped. I work in accounting. I might have spotted something wrong."

"We thought about it, but I was afraid to involve you. When someone sent Phil a blackmail text about a month ago, some of the group wanted to come stay here. The blackmailer told Phil to come to the inn, or they would call the reporters to give them the story. We wanted to know who sent the text.

"I'd already talked to Detective Zueger about the way Phil scammed people, and he's investigating. We didn't tell him everyone intended to come here.

"Of course, I work here, and I told them not to come." He stopped and glared at everyone around the table before continuing his story. "They were determined. I'm thinking the blackmailer knew I worked here. That's why he chose this place. We could sort of control..."

When he trailed off, Alex finished his sentence, "You could control the situation. And could either blackmail the truth out of him or threaten him."

"It wasn't supposed to turn out this way. No one was supposed to die." He scowled at Jade.

"You never said anything about weapons. I would never have killed him, and I didn't." She glared back. "You know Courtney and Alex took my gun away before anything happened to Phil."

Courtney interrupted their staring contest. "Obviously Jade had a relative scammed. Which other guests are part of this?"

Braden ducked his head again before raising it immediately. "Me, Jade, Rory, Melanie, Lauren."

Shock ran through her veins. "Everyone we have staying here?"

"Well, Phil bilked a lot of people."

"Essentially, every one of you is a suspect." Alex's voice came out hard and flat.

"I guess. Detective Zueger and Detective Entz know I work here. We might have failed to mention the blackmail text Phil received and other people whose relatives were scammed planned to come here. That's why I'm telling you in front of them." His face reddened as he nodded at the detective by the fireplace and Gary by the door. "No one was supposed to get hurt. We wanted proof. My mom lost a lot of money she didn't have to lose, and we thought we could get it back."

"Well, won't the police have fun sorting out who killed Phil? You all have the same motive and opportunity." Alex went back to the head of the table and sat down.

Courtney sensed Alex hid a host of hurt and betrayal by Braden. He needed to cool down to manage the situation. She wanted to get away from the group who threatened not only other guests, but also their business. "Alex, why don't we go to our office for a few minutes to discuss the situation with Nathan now we know what we're dealing with?"

Alex made a move to get up from the table, but Gary stepped forward. "It's best you all stay together until the sheriff and detective come back. Of course, you're all free to do what you want. No one is under arrest. It might be safer to stay together though."

Alex sat back down, pulling his phone out of his pocket. Courtney guessed he was texting Nathan. She knew Gary wouldn't want to be in the position of telling them what to do, since they'd helped him with his parents' case months ago. He had his deputy position to maintain, and she respected him enough to listen. Unless something came up she wanted to follow through on.

All their guests were suspects, and Braden had betrayed them both.

CHAPTER 14

Courtney grabbed food from the carts and pulled an empty chair over to sit beside Alex at the dining table as she waited impatiently for the sheriff and the detective from Minot to return.

"I'm going to go tell Willow she can start with the dishes," Courtney told Alex when she finished eating. The room had been mostly silent during the ten minutes she was eating. "Plus, I promised Kris tea. In all the commotion, I forgot."

After leaving the room and entering the kitchen, she briefly explained the situation to Willow while getting Kris's tea ready. Willow appeared shocked. She may have been the only one besides the owners who didn't know what was going on.

Courtney went to deliver the tea to Kris, along with a ham sandwich. When Kris opened the door, her eyes were red with bags beneath them.

"I've brought you the tea and a sandwich." She handed them to Kris. "Is there anything else I can do?"

"No. I'll be okay. I heard some shouting. Did they arrest Jade?" Kris asked as she put the tea and sandwich on the table by the window.

"Not yet. The situation is more complicated than we previously knew. As soon as I have more information, I'll let you know." Kris didn't need the additional strain of knowing the Minot Police had arrived. Had Kris known about the blackmail text Phil received? "If you need something else, let me know."

Kris nodded listlessly, and Courtney closed the door behind her as she left the room.

She returned to the great room and glanced around the table. Everyone slouched in their chairs except Hugh and Clarissa, who sat up straight. Hugh studied the contents of his coffee cup, and Clarissa's serene expression appeared pasted on.

They must all feel like hostages. She decided to move the gathering away from the table. Willow arrived, bringing another cart with tubs to ferry the dishes back to the kitchen. "Can the rest of you help Willow by taking your plates over to the cart? Once the table's cleared, we're going to move to the more comfortable seating areas. There's no sense in sitting uncomfortably at the table."

Everyone moved slowly at first, as if afraid one of the police would pull out his gun. Their shoulders relaxed as they cleared the table and moved into the various seating areas afterward.

Courtney sat across from Jade. "Are you okay?"

Jade stared at her as if she didn't understand the question.

"Are you afraid of the police because of your threat to Phil this morning?" Courtney asked, doing her own investigation while checking on her guests. She didn't know who to trust, other than Alex, Clarissa, and Hugh.

"No." Jade sat on the couch next to Melanie, her knees tucked up under her chin with her arms around them, her stockinged feet resting on the sofa. "As I said, you took the gun, and I have a permit."

"Where did you get a gun?" Courtney failed to remind her that having a permit didn't allow someone to wave the gun around and point it at people.

"My aunt inherited it from Uncle Hank. He was a gun collector, and she thought I might want a keepsake." She shuddered. "I didn't, but she insisted. How morbid. My uncle shot himself. Why would I want it for a keepsake? I got the permit I needed and planned to get rid of it at a pawn shop.

"I only brought it with me for protection. The quiet of the morning brought up all my anger at Phil's treatment of Uncle Hank. It was like someone took over my body. I grabbed the gun and rushed to the sunroom to yell at him. I was more shocked than he was." Biting her lip, she pulled her arms tighter around herself.

Courtney shivered.

"All of these people," Jade swept her arm across the sitting area, pointing at the group, "have the same motive, so I don't feel alone in having the finger aimed at me. I may not be the only one who brought a gun."

Courtney's eyes widened. Did someone else bring a gun, or were there a few guns hidden in their guests' rooms? "Okay. Who brought a gun?"

"Um." Detective Entz cleared his throat. "I don't believe you should be asking questions at this time."

Courtney stood up and glared at him, her cheeks flushed. She owned this inn and was within her rights to ask if her guests carried weapons. She and Alex should have checked after finding out about Jade's gun. She jumped when Alex put his hand on her shoulder, turning to find him right behind her.

He shook his head.

She studied him for a minute and decided not to make an enemy of the detective. The guests would probably lie to her anyway. They seemed to be quite capable of subterfuge. She turned her frown on them and sat down.

Her frown deepened as she realized all their guests were suspects, and their grand opening had turned into a grand failure. Instead of Crocus Hill Inn being a place to reset their life with A New Day Program, someone from the community would come up with a new name for their business meaning "death."

She nodded at Detective Entz. "Would you mind interviewing Clarissa and Hugh Alois first, so they can return to their house in Elm City? I saw Clarissa here all afternoon, and I'm sure she saw patients during the time in question.

"And Willow too? She's been in the kitchen cooking and doing dishes all day. She had no chance to leave and needs to be back tomorrow morning to feed everyone breakfast. Can you please ask Detective Zueger when he returns?" She poured on the charm with a wheedling voice.

"I'll pass the request on," Detective Entz agreed.

"Thank you." She turned to Alex. "How about we sit over there?" She pointed to the farthest corner, wanting distance from their guests.

Courtney asked Clarissa and Hugh to join them. Soon they were all seated, and Courtney relaxed next to Alex, trying to rein in her irritation at Braden. He had no choice if the others decided to stay here. However, he could have told them about Phil and everything else.

The enclosed sunroom door squeaked open, and the footsteps of Detective Zueger and Sheriff Warren sounded in the hallway.

CHAPTER 15

Sheriff Warren had clearly taken charge by the way he strode down the hallway slightly in front of Detective Zueger. Courtney watched their twin frowns as they studied the guests.

"I'll talk to you last." The sheriff glared at Braden.

"I wanted to tell you—"

Braden didn't get a chance to finish. Detective Zueger waved him off. Braden slumped back into the armchair. His frown didn't have the same effect as the detective's expression, and Coutney thought she detected a hint of tears.

"Jade. You're up first."

Jade threw an imploring look at Lauren and Melanie.

"It'll be okay. Tell him what we told Detective Zueger in Minot. If he asks anything pointing to you, tell him you want an attorney." Lauren crossed her arms around her middle but met the sheriff's gaze without flinching.

Courtney hadn't spent much time with Lauren but liked the young woman.

"Can I sit in on the interview?" Alex asked. "I feel one of us should know what's going on here." He started down the hallway, as if it were a given they would allow him to watch.

"No," Sheriff Warren said to Alex's retreating back.

Alex turned around and headed back to the great room.

"Courtney's joining us," the sheriff said.

"Thank you." Jade's voice rose over the sheriff's deep tones.

The sheriff motioned to Jade, ushering her in front of him. Courtney followed with the detective walking behind her. It wasn't quite what she hoped for when gathering the four of them in the corner. It was better. She could listen to the interview with Jade, while Alex could get Braden's version of the whole mess.

The sheriff and detective settled at one of the tables in the sunroom. The sheriff took out his pen and small notebook she recalled from the morning's interview. *Was that only this morning?* He also carried a briefcase and pulled out what looked like an index card and black ink. "Let's get your fingerprints on file."

Jade hugged herself as if cold, glancing nervously back and forth between the policemen. "Do I have to?"

"We need to have all the guests' fingerprints. You're first. If you got a gun permit, as you claim, your prints are already on file. Courtney's next." Sheriff Warren turned his blue gaze on her.

Courtney knew her shock over them asking for her prints made her look guilty.

"Routine," he said. "Or we can get a warrant."

Courtney shrugged, totally out of her depth. She knew the police would get a warrant anyway. "I'll go first. We may as well get this over with."

Jade's hands shook when they took her prints, but the sheriff held her finger steady when he pressed it on her card. He finished up the paperwork after getting each of their prints, stuffing them into his briefcase.

"We'd like to hear about your movements from 1:00 p.m. to 6:00 p.m. this afternoon," the sheriff told Jade.

Jade glanced at Courtney, who gave her an encouraging nod. This was not the same defiant woman from the morning.

"I ate with the rest of the group. After that, I went for a drive. I had an appointment with Dr. Alois at 1:30 p.m., so I came back about a half hour later. Lauren and I were together watching television. Then I saw Dr. Alois. When I came out, Lauren went to see her. Her appointment was at 2:00." She seemed to relax slightly as she recited her actions.

"You could have left after you saw Dr. Alois. Did you?" Sheriff Warren wrote a few notes on his pad.

"No. I stayed here." A hint of defiance returned.

Courtney was getting a bad taste in her mouth. Jade had time to get to Phil, if she wanted to.

"Why did you come to the inn, Ms. Nelson?" His steady gaze rested on her.

"I…well…you see, everyone decided it would be a good idea to come talk to Mr. Young." Her voice gathered momentum. "We thought if he saw us all in person, he'd be more likely to take us seriously and return the money."

The sheriff jotted down more notes. "What did he say when you asked him for the money?"

"We never had time to talk to him. The plan was to see him tonight after we ate." She grimaced.

"Yet you felt it necessary to threaten him this morning." The steel-blue eyes bored into her.

She turned a scared look toward Courtney. "I told you nothing happened. Phil also told you nothing happened."

"Yet, here we are. Only hours later, he's dead." He wasn't taking notes now but staring at her.

She squirmed. "How many times do I have to tell you…?" Her voice rose. "I didn't kill him. Someone else framed me!"

***

Alex wanted to talk to Braden. He glanced around the room. How could he talk to him without the deputy and the detective listening? There was no way. He might have to wait until the police left. He looked at the clock above their nook in the corner. Nine o'clock. It felt much later. "Will the police interview everyone tonight? It's going to take a long time."

"They have a great pool of suspects right here." Hugh patted his arm. "I would if I were them.

Especially if the Minot Police want to be part of the initial questioning. After these interviews, they'll leave the murder to the sheriff. This county is the sheriff's jurisdiction. The detectives will go back to Minot and continue with the fraud case."

"I wonder if they'll prosecute Kris. Maybe she didn't know what Phil was doing," Clarissa said.

"They'll have to find out if she knew or not." Alex tried to relax but found it nearly impossible. He kept remembering the questioning he'd gone through before they charged him with embezzlement three years ago. He hadn't done anything wrong then, and he didn't do anything wrong now.

"I've seen it happen where the wife didn't know what the husband was doing." Clarissa spoke from plenty of experience as a counselor.

Silence filled the room. Nobody talked, except them.

Lauren twirled her hair around her finger, a frown marring her smooth complexion. Melanie looked moodily down at the floor, while Braden leaned back in his chair, staring at the ceiling.

Rory and Ivy sat beside each other on one of the couches, holding hands while whispering to each other. Their pleasant expressions indicated they weren't worried about what happened.

Were they able to hide their feelings that well? Or didn't they care? They were the obvious suspects, considering they were the last to see Phil alive. They met him at the gun range, and then he was dead. They'd finally returned to the inn after the sheriff and deputy arrived.

Courtney had spent more time with the other guests than Alex. He'd hardly said more than hello to Rory and Ivy because the two always drove off to some new activity. He hadn't minded them being gone so much. He and Courtney hoped their guests would sightsee when they set up the inn near the Badlands and Medora. But their guests' time away from the inn made it harder to get to know them.

Alex decided to talk with the couple and ask where they'd been sightseeing when they left the gun range. When the sunroom door slammed open, he stood to see what was happening. He noticed the detective by the hallway edged around the corner to look.

"I'm done answering questions!" Jade screamed.

Alex couldn't see the hallway from the corner of the couch where he stood. But he could hear Courtney's soothing voice telling Jade it would be okay.

"No, it won't! They think I did it!"

Jade ran into the room, kicking Braden in the leg on her way past him. "It's all your fault. You're the one who started this whole thing by going to the police. You too." She stared at Lauren. "You and Braden. Thinking we were going to get our money back. Well, nothing's going to bring Hank back from the dead. I wish I'd never gotten involved with any of you!" Then she plopped down beside Melanie on the couch and started sobbing.

Melanie put her arm around Jade, patting her on the back. She murmured as Jade cried hysterically.

Braden rubbed his shin.

CHAPTER 16

Courtney followed Jade into the room, settling back in the corner with Alex, Clarissa and Hugh. The sheriff and detective remained behind, probably conferring. She watched Braden's shoulders slump further.

She'd learned nothing from the interview the sheriff conducted with Jade. It was a repeat of the earlier threats Jade made against Phil, and when Alex and Courtney discovered her handing the gun off to Skylar.

"You got us into this, Braden." Jade finally took a breath without crying. "It's all your fault. You better get us out of it. I can't afford to miss work and be questioned by the police. What if I lose my job?"

At the pronouncement, Braden sat up straight, his shoulders square with his body. He stared over Melanie's shoulder at Jade. "I never told you to bring a weapon. You brought this on yourself.

"Plus, I'm not the one who started this whole thing about coming to the inn. That was someone else's idea. I said I worked here, and suddenly someone decided to send Phil a blackmail text to come here. I certainly didn't want you all here. The police were managing it. Don't blame me.

Blame whoever sent the text." He slumped back against the cushion.

A choking sound came from the hallway. They all looked over to see Kris standing in the doorway leading to the guests' rooms. Her hand covered her mouth as she stared at them in shock.

Lauren jumped up and ran over to Kris. "It's not your fault, Aunt Kris. You couldn't have known someone would kill Uncle Phil." She hugged Kris to her.

Kris stood there. Tears streamed down her face.

They were related? Courtney wasn't the only one astonished at the news. Most of the others in the room appeared surprised.

After the first shock wore off, Courtney saw Kris wobble as she leaned against the wall. She rushed over to assist Lauren, who urged Kris to go back to her room.

"Get some rest," Lauren said. "We can sort this out tomorrow."

"I can't," Kris whispered. "I can't wait until tomorrow. The police are here now." Her gaze landed on Detective Entz, who listened to the exchange without interfering. "He knows everything."

Gary frowned. Courtney decided he wasn't in the loop like the Minot Police. She knew he wouldn't like that, but the sheriff had been taken by surprise too.

"Not quite everything, Mrs. Young. I don't know who killed your husband," Detective Entz disagreed.

"I didn't mean that." Kris's tone held a haughty note, impressing Courtney by the change in her demeanor. Despite her grief, her backbone remained in place.

Melanie stood up and stared at Lauren. "You never told us Phil was your uncle."

A general murmur of annoyance came from the others in the room.

"I have the same grievance you have. Uncle Phil stole money from me. When I told Aunt Kris what I knew, she agreed to come when Uncle Phil got the blackmail text. She wanted to know which one of you sent it." Lauren stared at them with her head held high.

Braden got up and paced behind the couch, looking at Kris. "So, you told Lauren to continue the secrecy about her relationship with you. What were you going to do when you found out who the blackmailer was? Were you going to have them arrested, giving Phil up to the police? I doubt it."

He glared at Lauren. "Everybody kept blaming me. I can't believe you're their niece but never told us. Traitor."

"The detectives knew. They didn't see anything wrong with it," Lauren said.

Kris moved farther into the room and settled on the armchair closest to Detective Entz. Lauren went back to her armchair, while her former cohorts glared at her.

Courtney sighed to herself. All her guests were turning against each other, and one of them was a murderer. *Lovely. Just lovely.* Was Alex having as much fun as she was? More importantly, would someone else be killed? Were they all in danger?

CHAPTER 17

Courtney stood beside Kris's chair, her sympathy tinged with anger. The woman's husband was dead, but she'd known about the blackmail. "I don't understand what you hoped to gain. If the police knew something of his scams, why did you need to keep the blackmail a secret?"

Detective Entz took a step toward them. "Enough talking about this until we have everyone's statements. Mrs. Richmond, I suggest you find something else to do. The rest of you too."

Courtney glared at him. Even if Phil scammed people, he didn't deserve to be killed. Also, her inn's reputation hinged on good will and relaxed and happy times. "Fine," she huffed and started walking back to the corner by Hugh and Clarissa. The sound of Braden's boots clomping on the wood floor behind the sofa changed her mind.

She turned around and went back to the group. "We're not going to sit around and mope. Lauren, can you write in the corner over there?" She pointed to a recliner away from the group by the television room, opposite Hugh and Clarissa's corner.

"If I had my laptop. I do have a deadline. I could try and write." She seemed unsure how successful she'd be, but her demeanor brightened.

"Okay. Go to your room and get your laptop. Detective Entz will be happy to escort you. I'm sure he doesn't want you roaming the hall by yourself." She smiled sweetly at the detective.

His eyes narrowed, but he nodded. Getting his charges involved in something other than sniping at each other would probably be a relief.

While they went to Lauren's room to get her laptop, Courtney turned to Braden. "Willow must be incredibly tired by now. You get to help with kitchen duty. I can tell by your pacing, sitting down isn't going to be easy for you."

At the mention of Willow, his face lit up. "Sure. Whatever she needs."

She motioned for him to follow her. When she met Lauren and the detective in the hallway, she explained Braden would be with Willow in the kitchen.

"Please go back to the great room and sit down," the detective told Lauren.

She frowned behind his back but continued down the hallway. As Gary at the front door had a perfect view of the hallway, her frown didn't go unnoticed, but the whole group was unhappy.

The detective followed Courtney and Braden into the kitchen.

"I've brought you some help," Courtney told Willow.

Willow's arms were up to the elbows in suds in the kitchen sink as she washed some pans. She turned her head around far enough to see Braden and shrugged. "If he's the best you can do, I'd better do it myself."

"Funny." But the light in his eyes dimmed slightly.

She smiled and turned back to the sink. "Thank you, Braden. I need to get some things done to prepare for breakfast tomorrow. There are three cartons of eggs in the fridge. Why don't you get them out and start cracking?"

Courtney left them to it.

The detective followed her out of the kitchen area and past the sitting room area. "This is quite the place you have here. This sitting area is perfect for relaxing."

"On the weekends, we don't use the great room. We use this room. Plus, it gives Willow a place to relax when she can. Unfortunately, as this is our first week in business, she hasn't established a routine yet. Trying to cook for all these people and learn the ropes while juggling interviews and police and grieving guests is a bit much. I'm going to have to see if Skylar can come work full-time for the rest of the week."

She glanced at the clock on the wall. *Ten.* Maybe she should text Skylar and ask her if she could work every day for the rest of the week.

The detective stood in the sitting room area looking around. "Was Skylar here today?"

"Until one. She got everything ready yesterday, so the guests didn't need much this morning. She helped Willow and left when everything was under control."

"I'll have to interview her," Detective Entz said.

Courtney pulled her phone out of her back jeans pocket. "I want her to work the rest of the week if she's available, so I can give you the information right now." She gave the detective Skylar's phone number and address, then sent her a brief text message.

"Did you tell her anything?" His lips pressed together.

"No, I did not. I asked if she could work all day for the rest of the week."

A ding sounded on her phone.

Courtney looked at the device. "She said yes."

His lips relaxed, and his shoulders dropped. "Okay. Back to the others. I hope you have something else for each of them to do." He grinned at her.

"As long as they don't go too far, right?" she asked.

"Right. But no one's under arrest, so they are free to do what they want."

Like anyone would feel free to do what they wanted. She didn't believe they would. They all felt under house arrest with the police here. Not one law officer but four. But their presence was actually a relief to Courtney with a murderer on the loose. A murderer who was probably one of her guests. But which one?

CHAPTER 18

When Courtney returned to the great room, she managed to convince Kris to go back to her room. The hostility against her vibrated off the walls.

Jade curled up on the corner of the couch with her eyes closed, and Melanie pulled a book from the shelf near her and started reading—the book Phil read the previous day and earlier this morning.

Courtney joined Clarissa and Hugh again, even though she wanted to check on Alex. He'd been with the sheriff and detective a long time since they'd finished questioning Jade.

Nothing new came from Jade's questioning, except she didn't have a solid alibi. Jade could go back to her room but decided to stay with the rest of them.

The crunch of gravel sounded on the drive outside. She only expected Nathan, and he couldn't have possibly made it this soon. Not unless he dropped everything the minute they first contacted him.

Because it was dark outside, they couldn't see who drove up. Alex would have to add motion sensor lights in the area. Detective Entz joined Deputy Lachlan at the door.

Courtney found herself ready to giggle and realized how tired she was. When she got this exhausted, everything seemed funny.

Did they think a shooter would drive up and come in guns blazing? It turned out to be Deputy Lachlan's replacement, Deputy Simons. After a brief exchange, he sat in the seat Gary vacated.

She stepped outside to talk to Gary. "How are you doing?"

He winked at her. "Peachy. How does it feel to be in on a murder again?"

His easygoing attitude relaxed her, and she let out a brief laugh. "Not so hot. One of my guests is probably a killer." Suddenly, her giggles ended, and a spurt of anger took its place. "My dream inn. And Braden…"

"Yes. I know you must feel betrayed." Gary placed his hand on her arm. "We'll find the person soon. I promise."

She sighed. "I hope."

"How about praying?" Gary winked at her again.

She barely caught his expression from the dim light shining through the screen door. "You should teach one of Hugh's classes on spirituality."

"I'm not sure that would be a good idea." He studied her expression. "But maybe sometime I could give a talk on why I started questioning God and where that led."

Excitement bubbled up inside her. A nice contrast to how she'd felt since finding out her dream inn had a murderer. This was the kind of moment she'd hoped for when she started the inn.

"Great. I'll let you go. I'm sure I'll see you around in the next few days."

"Definitely." He patted her arm again before walking down to the car Deputy Simons had driven up in.

She went back inside, buoyed by Gary's potential as a speaker. She saw Clarissa's gaze on her and wasn't surprised when she gestured to Courtney to join them.

"Go get Alex," Clarissa said, voicing Courtney's disquiet. "I'm wondering what's taking them so long to ask him questions."

Alex had been with the detective and sheriff a long time since Jade returned. They were questioning him as a suspect. Courtney reached out and touched Clarissa's hand. "Thank you."

She hurried in the direction of the hallway and rushed to the sunroom door, ignoring Detective Entz, who followed behind her, telling her to stop. She refused to stop.

She stepped into the sunroom and took in Alex's tight expression in one glance. Their eyes met. "You've been answering their questions long enough."

He paused for only a moment, and then said, "I'm done answering questions for now. I believe I've told you my movements and what I discovered when I found Phil." He stood up from the table, where he'd been sitting across from the lawmen.

"Why are you questioning him?" Courtney asked the sheriff.

"We wanted him to tell us about finding Mr. Young. We were getting more detail of what he saw."

Surprised he answered, she supposed he realized she would get the whole story from Alex anyway. "It took you a long time to hear he drove around, found the body, and waited for your people. He could have driven away without reporting it if he wanted to hide something. Besides, he was at the inn all afternoon with Braden, me, and Clarissa as witnesses. He didn't leave." She turned around to follow Alex from the room.

"We aren't done asking questions," the sheriff warned.

They ignored the sheriff's annoyed expression as they went to their office. Alex tried to key in the code to the door, but his hand shook too badly.

Courtney reached around him and punched in the numbers, then turned the knob. Soon they stood in the office with all their problems on the other side of the door. She stepped into his space and wrapped her arms around him.

"It's okay," she whispered. She knew he'd been taken back in time to when they questioned him about stealing money from the bank. A crime he hadn't committed, but it didn't make a difference in the outcome. He'd spent two years in jail and feared going back. She knew being with the police so long triggered some memories.

He put his arms around her and held her. He didn't say anything.

They stood there until his trembling ceased. A few minutes later, he let her go, and she released him and took a step back. His forehead smoothed out, and his lips weren't pressed together anymore.

"Let's sit down." She moved her chair over to his as soon as he sat, and she took one of his hands in hers. "We're going to hide out here until Nathan comes."

"What about our guests?" he asked.

"They brought this on themselves. Braden knows where everything is and can take care of them. I am so mad at him right now."

Alex nodded and let out a weary sigh. "Yeah."

A knock sounded, and they looked at each other, both smiling as they ignored it. Clarissa or Hugh would text them if they needed something. The police might be upset if they wanted something. She didn't care. They could go through Braden or text their question.

CHAPTER 19

A deep voice came from the other side of the door, "Hey! It's Nathan!"

Courtney smiled at Alex, jumped up and hurried to the door. Relief coursed through her whole body. She felt limp as she opened the door, saw her brother and pulled him into the room. His hug warmed her from the inside out as she sighed. "Thank goodness you're here."

He released her and stepped over to Alex, and they shook hands. "Good to see you, Nathan. It's been crazy here, as you've probably guessed."

"I'm glad you called me this time, and we can get this taken care of properly." Nathan set his briefcase on a side table and pulled up another chair, so the three of them sat in triangle formation. "We're going to have to jump right into the necessities. You can fill me in on the rest of the story later. Have they questioned either one of you?"

"They asked me what I did this afternoon," Courtney said. "I have an alibi for the right time with enough witnesses. I never left the property. I'm pretty much in the clear. Alex, not so much." Thank goodness she could share this fear with Nathan this time around.

"What's the time frame?"

"Phil left the inn around 1:00 p.m., and Alex found him around 5:30 p.m.," Courtney answered.

Alex absently studied a hangnail on his finger. "We should have sent Braden to look for him." The animosity in his voice lingered in the air.

"Got a thing against Braden?" Nathan met him when he'd come to see the inn being built.

"Well, he did gather a bunch of people into a revenge group, bring them to the inn, and set them loose to kill Phil," Alex said bitterly, rubbing his forehead.

"Maybe," Courtney said. "While they were questioning Alex, I found out Lauren, one of the guests, is Phil's niece. Phil scammed her out of money too. The short story of this whole debacle is Phil scammed Lauren and Rory, and the rest of the guests are younger members of the families trying to get Phil arrested and get their money back. Someone sent Phil a blackmail text to come to the inn. If he didn't come, they would tell the police or reporters. Now we know Lauren is his niece, it's possible he already knew about the police being involved. Which sums up the highlights."

"Okay. We'll get into details later. I'm going to have to ask you to leave, Courtney, so what Alex and I discuss can be under lawyer privilege."

"He's going to tell me what you talk about and his interrogation anyway." Courtney didn't want to leave Alex. His expression when she'd interrupted the police scared her. He'd been traumatized.

"Sorry, Sis." Nathan pointed at the door.

Alex got up and hugged her where she sat in her chair. "Go, honey. Nathan's got this."

"I promise not to leave his side," Nathan assured her.

She finally got up, kissed Alex on the lips, and then Nathan on the cheek. "Good to see you, Nathan."

She reluctantly walked to the door. "Okay. I'm going upstairs to our apartment after I make sure Clarissa and Hugh are taken care of. I'm putting Braden in charge. As soon as Willow is done, she needs you to follow her home. Can you guys do it? I don't want her driving alone tonight."

"Sure. We'll take care of it." Strength returned to Alex's voice.

Nathan was with him, and Alex had recovered his equilibrium. "I'll let Willow know, and I'll see you later. Text if I'm needed." She paused at the door and rested her head on it.

"Go," Alex said softly.

She nodded and slipped out of the room.

CHAPTER 20

Courtney went back to the great room and stopped next to Detective Entz, who had found a chair and now sat in the area where he'd been standing by the hallway. The atmosphere in the room signaled no one had any energy left to make a run for it, but Deputy Simons sat by the door looking young and alert.

"Who are they interviewing now?" she asked the detective.

"Willow."

"Okay. Thank you."

He nodded.

She glanced around the room and spoke to anybody listening, "I'm going to my room upstairs. Alex is with his attorney. The rest of you can go to your rooms as soon as the police are done questioning you. We'll meet here tomorrow morning at 9:00 a.m. for breakfast and to discuss the rest of the week, depending on what the police have in mind, and what you want to do."

She looked at Braden, who'd been listening closely to her. "You're in charge for the rest of the night. Text Alex or myself if there's a problem. You might as well lock up everything except the front door right now. Alex and Nathan are following Willow home later and will lock up the front area then."

She gazed at Deputy Simon. "I'm assuming you're planted there for the night?"

He nodded.

"So, the deputy has a clear view of the hallway. You're all safe for the night. He can see everyone who leaves their room."

She finished her rounds by thanking Clarissa and Hugh and telling them to text her if they needed anything, code for letting her and Alex know if something important happened. Then she finally went down the hallway to the staircase near the enclosed sunroom.

She suddenly remembered Willow. She opened the sunroom door and poked her head in to see Willow sitting across from the sheriff and detective. "Willow, knock on the office door when you're done, and Alex and Nathan will follow you home. We don't want you driving alone tonight. What time do you plan to be here in the morning?"

Willow answered readily, "Six. Braden and I got a lot prepped tonight."

"Great. Thank you. Check in with Alex or me when you get here. Good night." She ignored law enforcement and went upstairs to her apartment. Probably not wise to antagonize those in charge, but her anger lingered. Thank goodness Nathan was here. Knowing he could be with Alex at every police interview comforted her.

She doubted if she would fall asleep when she got upstairs, but she sank onto the bed and lay there fully clothed, looking at the ceiling and trying to calm down. She wanted to know what Nathan and Alex were discussing. And who killed Phil. And

what would happen tomorrow? She couldn't begin
to guess.

CHAPTER 21
Tuesday Morning

Courtney heard the chime on her phone the next morning and rolled over in bed to glance at who texted. Willow. She had arrived in the kitchen. After returning a thumbs-up emoji, she slid out of bed and glanced at Alex.

Sound asleep, the lines in his face relaxed, he looked younger and defenseless. What bad luck he found Phil's body, which made him a suspect. Why couldn't the police have discovered the scene first?

Alex's plan had been to stay home and work on the books in the afternoon, not go driving around the countryside searching for a lost guest. She wanted to scream in frustration at only a little past six. She needed to keep her temper in check with their guests for the rest of the day.

Why did the police question Alex? He had no motive. Maybe to kill Braden for the whole fiasco, but not Phil. She needed to find out what they focused on in the interview with her husband.

She showered and dressed. While she put on her shoes, Alex rolled over in bed. "Good morning," he rasped.

"Good morning." She leaned over the bed and kissed him. "How are you?"

"Tired." He laughed. "Nathan and I were up late."

"You can go back to sleep if you want. I can take care of things for a while. I have Braden, and Nathan will pitch in. He's up early. He's never needed much sleep. He's probably even been out for a run around the property, showered and dressed already."

"I'm going to get up and get ready." He slid up and leaned against the headboard.

"Can I ask about the police questioning you?" She didn't want to cause him more pain, but she wanted to know, so she could reassure him he had nothing to worry about in relation to Phil's death.

"Sure." He grimaced. "They were intent on finding out what time I found Phil. I told them, but they kept asking me. Then they wanted to know if I'd met him before he became a guest. I told them I hadn't ever seen him and only knew what he'd put on his application for the week's stay. I don't know why they kept asking me those same questions, in different ways, over and over. Thank goodness you came when you did, because I was about ready to jump up and scream. I told them to ask Braden. He seemed to know everything."

She heard the bitterness at the end of the sentence. "I'm sorry about Braden. When this is over, we're going to have to decide what to do about him. We know he didn't kill Phil because he was here all afternoon, but he kept a big secret from us."

"I know. One thing at a time." He smiled at her. "Anything else?"

"No." She smiled back. "I guess we better put on our armor and get through this day. I said extra prayers in the shower. God will be hearing from me often today."

He nodded. "Me too."

She finished tying her shoe and stood up. "See you downstairs but don't hurry."

"I'll take my time. Text me if you need something."

She went around the bed and kissed him again, then headed downstairs to see what was going on. She found Deputy Lachlan in place, and Deputy Simons gone. She waved at Gary, who waved back. Both Detective Entz and Zueger were also gone.

"Good morning," she said to the deputy.

"Hi. You're up early." He smiled at her from his seat by the kitchen table.

"Have to make sure everything is ready for the day." She saw his to-go coffee cup on the table. "Do you need a refill?"

"Sure."

"It'll take me a few minutes to make coffee. Do you put anything in it?"

"Black. Thanks."

She made the coffee and refilled his cup. "I'm going to go talk to Willow. Do you want something to eat?"

"No. I'm good until nine." His smile expanded. "I hear everyone's meeting then."

She blushed and smiled back. "I did order everyone to attend. I meant guests, but you and any other law enforcement staff are welcome. Willow's a great cook. You won't be disappointed."

He nodded. "Sounds good. The sheriff and the detectives will be here to talk to you and Mr. Richmond before we eat."

"Okay. We'll be in our office." She headed back down the hallway to check if Willow needed her and met Alex on the way. He must have decided not to waste any time getting ready after she left the room, because his hair was wet. "There's coffee in the small kitchen."

He gave her a quick kiss. "Thanks, honey. I'll see you in the office as soon as I get some."

Courtney went into the big kitchen, where Willow stood by the stove, stirring something in a skillet. Courtney peeked over her shoulder, smelling melted sugar and cinnamon. "Yum."

"Glaze for the rolls," Willow said.

Courtney backed away from the stove and leaned against the counter. "So, I bet you heard some of what happened yesterday."

Willow's brown eyes darkened, and a furrow appeared on her forehead. "Someone killed Mr. Young. Braden filled me in and told me the plan he and the other guests put in place to get Phil to confess to what he'd done and to get some of the money back.

"Jade, Rory, and Braden gathered at a restaurant when they heard about the blackmail text, and the plan changed. They all came to find the identity of the blackmailer and get money back from Phil. I guess they thought, if they all came here, they could figure it out." Willow stirred the contents in the skillet.

"You know as much as I do. Alex and I haven't discussed the situation with Braden. The police interviewed him, and then Nathan and Alex talked. I went to bed." She felt guilty about falling asleep before Alex returned from following Willow home, but exhaustion claimed her. "Do you like Braden?"

Willow turned her face away from Courtney. "A little."

"I don't want to tell you what to do, but be careful. I'm having a few trust issues with Braden because of this situation. He did not share the information he should have with Alex and myself. Especially when our inn suddenly became a meeting place. I guess, before that, it was his personal business."

Willow shifted from one foot to the other and stared at the glaze as she stirred.

"That's all I'm going to say on the subject. You're a grown woman. Do you need any help this morning?"

Willow glanced at her. "Not right now. When it's time to cart the food into the other area."

"Text Alex and me. Braden needs to get the yard done for the wedding, or I'd put him in here to help you. Skylar should be here around ten to clean, unless she wants to eat with us at nine. If I were her, I'd steer clear of the nine o'clock meeting, but she needs to know what's going on too. The police may not want her to clean individual rooms if they decide to get a search warrant for anyone's room."

Willow's mouth opened and closed before she asked, "Search?"

"For anything incriminating." She didn't explain the murder weapon had been found with the body. "I'd better go talk to Alex before we're interrupted." She knew Nathan would join them, which was okay.

She texted Skylar about the breakfast meeting. She added the police would be present and have questions for her. The Elm City grapevine no doubt already informed Skylar of Phil's death, and Jade probably talked to her too. She'd call Skylar and update her as soon as she talked with Alex.

When she typed the code into their office door and opened it, she wasn't surprised to see Nathan sitting across from Alex at their worktable. He had coffee. "Do you need something to eat?"

"Nope. Already had a breakfast bar. I'll be fine until this big shindig in a few hours." He grinned at her and rubbed his hands together. "Okay. I know the two of you are on edge because of what happened to Phil, but there's no motive for Alex, so try and relax."

"Okay, Big Brother. It's too bad you're not married. You'd understand my worry more if you were." She plopped down in a vacant chair by the table.

"I know it's going to work out, because I'm here." His grin morphed into concern. "I'm sorry. There's an inn full of potential suspects, and Alex is innocent."

"Some of them have alibis," Alex spoke up and took a sip of coffee.

"Not all of them, Alex. We'll find the real murderer. This will be over, and you'll be celebrating your brother's wedding before you know it," Courtney said.

"In which case, Braden better not be the murderer. I need the yard ready," Alex joked. "Guess we'll have to keep him employed until after the wedding."

Courtney stood behind him and massaged his neck. "Nathan will pay for the yard to be done if he's wrong." She sent a worried look at her brother over Alex's head.

"Definitely. I keep a retinue of lawn workers ready at a moment's notice." He patted Alex's hand that didn't hold his coffee cup. Then he punched him in the shoulder. "Buck up."

Alex grinned in response, and the wrinkles on his forehead disappeared. "Right. Let's get this done. We can figure out what happened."

"Let's go over the police questions one more time."

Alex rolled his eyes at Nathan.

"I know. Repetition, boring ground covered. So, let's get it over with. One more time. I'm trying to figure out why they looked at you so closely when they have a whole bunch of other people to question." Nathan pulled some notes out of a briefcase.

"They wanted to know what I did with my afternoon. I'm covered, because we were out talking to Braden for a while, and I didn't leave the house until Kris called. They spent more time asking if I'd known why everybody came to see Phil. They thought there had to be some connection between me and Phil and kept harping on the point. I kept reminding Detective Zueger he'd been working with Braden and knew more than I did. I don't know why they kept asking me questions. I was glad when you interrupted." He put his hand over Courtney's where it lay on the table.

"Doing my wifely duty of keeping you free to help out here. Besides, now Nathan is here, he'll have everything sorted out with your alibi and the police, and they'll take you off their list." She smoothed his hair down where it stuck up slightly in back. "What else is going on? I missed whatever happened when I went to bed. Did you ever get a private word with Braden?"

CHAPTER 22

Alex glanced between Courtney and Nathan. "We didn't catch up with Braden. By the time we finished talking, he'd been interviewed and gone to his room. I thought about knocking but decided to wait until today to talk to him, so I wouldn't punch him. Plus, I was exhausted and not in a good mood."

"Good catch," Nathan said. "We don't need you showing any temper."

"So, who do you think did this?" She glanced back and forth between the guys.

"No idea at this point. They all have a motive," Alex said.

Nathan shrugged.

"Helpful." She stood up and took three blank sheets out of the ream of paper on the printer. After picking up a black fine-tip pen, she rejoined them at the conference table.

She wrote "Clear" on one page, "Maybe" on another page, and "Definite Suspects" on the third page. "We're starting a list."

"Obviously." Alex laughed.

She grinned. At least he'd relaxed since she'd come into the room. She wrote quickly and then showed the lists to them.

On the "Clear" page, she wrote:
Alex – no motive, alibi for most of the day

Courtney – alibi and no motive

Nathan – no known motive

Clarissa – no motive and has alibi

Hugh – no motive and ask if he has alibi

Willow – no known motive and has alibi (check for sure, but busy and vehicle didn't leave parking lot)

On the "Possible" list she wrote:

Skylar – Jade's "almost" cousin and another of Hank's nieces, not at work, opportunity

Braden – motive (mother lost money) and opportunity before he picked up Kris, but not much time, depends on time of death, which might have been before Braden left inn

On the "Definite Suspect" list she wrote:

Kris – motive (money and ??) and opportunity, last known person to see Phil alive

Lauren – motive (lost her own money) and opportunity, Phil is her uncle

Jade – motive (Uncle Hank suicide), opportunity, gun and threatened him

Melanie – motive (godmother lost money) and opportunity

Rory – motive (lost money), opportunity, and last to see Phil alive aside from Kris

Ivy – motive (lost money), opportunity, and last to see Phil alive aside from Kris

She showed the finished lists to Nathan and Alex, and they looked them over.

"A good summation." Nathan admired her notes. "Do we have everyone here this week listed?"

"I think so. We don't know if one of the guests or someone else sent him the blackmail text."

"I'd sure like to know who sent Phil the text getting him to the inn. No doubt our killer. The plan was excellent. Get all the suspects together, so he or she wasn't the only obvious person." Nathan frowned as he thought about it.

"I wondered the same thing. Kris didn't warn him to stay away." Courtney found that odd. "When I greeted them outside, Kris was enthusiastic and made some comment about walking in the countryside. Phil was annoyed we were far from a town or city. Three miles to Elm City isn't far, but I guess he meant bigger city life. Kris told us Phil convinced her to come here, so, despite the lack of amenities, he wanted to know who sent him the text. That must be why he came. Nothing else makes sense."

They sat thinking for a while.

"Would Braden send a blackmail text?" Nathan drew circles on the page in front of him.

"As angry as I am about Braden, let's assume he's clear because of his alibi," Alex said. "Kris, Lauren, and the rest of them knew the score. In fact, the Minot Police were in on the deal to catch Phil at something illegal."

"Well, they didn't send him an anonymous text," Nathan said.

"Spoken like a true lawyer, Big Brother." Though she was appalled at the idea the police might have set the whole thing into operation, she knew Nathan was joking.

"We aren't going to find out by sitting in here discussing things. We need more information, so we should set up a plan." Courtney stood up and gathered the papers together. "I'm searching all the rooms today."

"You can't." Nathan held up a hand to stop her.

"I'm an innkeeper. People need towels and who knows what else. They'll each be taking their time away from here. I can guarantee you, as soon as breakfast is over," she quickly glanced at her phone—fifteen minutes to go, "they'll all be out wandering the countryside. If they don't pack up and leave."

"They'll want to know what's happening, and they'd look guilty if they left." Nathan stood up too. "I would, anyway. I'll see what information I can get from the guests. I can get one or two of them to talk to me."

"You always want to know everything." She grinned at him despite the circumstances. "You always have."

"Makes me a great lawyer." He swung his arm around her shoulders and pulled her to him in a quick hug.

"Hey. What about me?" Alex finally pushed his chair away from the table and stood up too.

"You capture Braden and get a full accounting of what brought everyone here. Then come back, look at this list and see who else we can talk to about their alibis. We can leave notes on these papers." She picked them up and shoved them in her right desk drawer. "I'm putting them here in case someone happens to be in the room and glances around."

"Thank goodness we're the only ones with the code to the room, so no one can snoop," Alex agreed.

Courtney looked at Nathan. "Good call on your part. And the siren going off if the wrong code is entered is great. That'll scare anyone trying to come in without our escort." She wished someone would—then it would be easy to catch the killer.

"Breakfast time." Nathan rubbed his stomach and smiled through even white teeth. "We've got work to do."

Alex didn't look as excited at the prospect as Nathan, and Courtney had a sick feeling in the pit of her stomach at meeting with their guests and possibly the police. Ever since Alex spent time in prison for embezzling, he'd been nervous around any law enforcement officers. Even though he was innocent, he took the blame for a friend who had cancer. The two years in prison changed him.

CHAPTER 23

Rory caught up to them as they stepped into the hallway. Was he trying to listen to their conversation? They'd spoken in low voices, and the room was almost soundproofed anyway.

"I'm wondering about a refund for the week." Rory blocked the hallway with his bulky frame. He was about the same height as Alex, but Nathan, standing a few inches taller, looked down at him.

"We haven't made up our mind what's going to happen yet," Nathan answered for them.

Thank goodness for his quick thinking. Courtney hadn't considered someone might want a refund. This group staying purposely brought the enemy with them.

"I didn't come here for someone to get murdered on my vacation." His voice trembled with indignation.

"You lost money, Rory. You're a suspect. Until we know who killed Phil Young, we're not discussing refunds with anyone," Alex said. "I'm assuming the police have arrived, and we're about to have breakfast, so if you'll let us past to join them…"

Rory knew when to quit and let them pass, following them into the great room.

Alex was right. The Minot police and Sheriff Warren sat at the end of the dining table, along with Deputy Gary Lachlan.

Skylar sat on one of the armchairs in the corner of the room. Courtney told her, "I'll fill you in on what's going on as soon as we've finished breakfast, and I can get away."

"Willow and I talked this morning when I arrived. She told me. I also talked to Jade. Do you want me to clean as planned?" Skylar didn't show any concern over the events. *Odd.*

"Start with this area after you've helped Willow clear the dishes from the table. I'll go with you to the individual rooms when you vacuum and get them anything they need. I don't know if any of the guests will leave after breakfast, but I'll tell you how to proceed once we find out what's going on."

Courtney had every intention of snooping. Uneasy about the possibility of other weapons and her guests' dishonesty, she was determined to search while Skylar cleaned, hiding her real motive.

Skylar nodded. "Sure."

"Can you go help Willow bring in the food? It's time to get this started."

"This." Skylar grinned. "Whatever this is."

"Exactly." At least someone found the situation amusing.

As Willow and Skylar brought in the food, the guests took their places at the table, filling in between the police and Alex. The police sat at the far end of the table, and Alex and Courtney were at their usual places at the head of the table. Nathan sat on Alex's right. Clarissa and Hugh already left for their duties in Elm City.

With everyone sitting there, the table suddenly seemed smaller than usual, even though there were a few empty places, places Willow and Skylar would sit when they finished their duties. Unfortunately, they were both going to be sitting beside the police on either side of the table.

Courtney almost moved herself and Alex down to sit there but decided the police encroaching on the table might be a good thing. The innocent among them would be uncomfortable, but, hopefully, so would the murderer. She didn't expect a spontaneous confession though.

The oppressive atmosphere eased slightly as everyone started eating. Courtney decided not to eat anything but put a few scrambled eggs and a token slice of toast on her plate while they all sat there. She and Alex were going to be setting some ground rules. She could eat after they finished.

She stood up. Everyone paused, forks poised halfway to mouths when she started talking. "I know this is uncomfortable for everyone. I can't make you talk to the psychologist in residence, Dr. Clarissa Alois, but you'll all have an appointment with her this afternoon when she returns. The schedule is on the bulletin board. I expect you to show up at her office on time. If you don't want to talk, then sit there in silence, but you will appear in her office. I don't want it said I neglected your mental health when you've all been exposed to this trauma.

"As far as the rest of the day's events, I'm going to let the police tell you what's going to happen and what they want us to do."

"You can't force us to stay," Rory spoke up—which explained why he wanted a refund. He planned to leave with Ivy.

"You're right; we can't. Perhaps one of the detectives would like to address the issue?"

Sheriff Warren stood up too. "No one is under arrest at this time and can leave at any time, but…"

Braden interrupted him, "We're all suspects."

The sheriff studied him for a moment. "Almost all of you are. There are a few exceptions due to alibis, but I have something else to say."

He looked around at everyone. "You've already paid for the week. You're here. Why don't you stay?" He looked around the great room. "It seems like a comfortable place to stay. There are attractions in the towns around here. You're all free to come and go…at this time.

"That said, we do want to clarify things with each of you this morning, and then Detective Entz and Detective Zueger will be returning to Minot. The investigation will be ongoing, and if you have further information, please let us know this morning, or whenever it occurs to you. We'll give you contact information. Braden will no longer be your contact. His purpose has been served."

Braden's face turned bright red.

Courtney wasn't sure if he felt insulted or not. If Braden hadn't gotten them together at the inn, he was an innocent bystander who'd been used. She softened toward him before reminding herself she didn't know his role in the events.

"So, we're going to let you finish eating, and Detective Entz will let you know when it's your turn to join us in the sunroom again. Deputy Lachlan will be leaving now."

Gary stood up and laid a business card on the table. "Thank you, Courtney and Alex. If any of you need something, please call."

He escaped out the front door before Courtney or Alex could respond. Nathan hid a grin. What amused him? She had no idea. She knew how to reach Gary if she wanted to talk to him. "Do you want an escort to the sunroom?"

"No, thanks," Detective Zueger said. "We can find our way. Braden, you're up first. Give us five minutes and then please join us."

Braden's face paled, and he set his fork down.

"You can go back to working on the yard as soon as they're done with you," Alex told him.

Braden nodded. Would Alex and Nathan join Braden as soon as he returned to the yard?

The police disappeared down the hallway, and they heard the sunroom door open and close. The slight relaxation of tense shoulders and a few sighs ran through the room. Everyone suddenly had an appetite and ate faster.

Courtney sat down and ate the few eggs on her plate and nibbled at her toast. Braden left to be interviewed, and, one by one, the other guests left the table. Some went to their rooms, and some settled in the great room. Soon Nathan, Alex, Courtney, Willow, and Skylar remained at the table.

"Thanks for everything, Willow," Courtney said. "I know it's been an inconvenience to eat with us and cook. Sounds like the police will be gone by noon, so you'll be free to work without interruption. When you want Skylar's help, tell me, and I'll find her for you.

"Skylar, thanks for being flexible to work full days for the rest of the week. Hopefully, this will be a one-time thing."

Skylar laughed. "I'm finding it almost fun—except for being a suspect."

At their stunned look, she said, "Not much has happened in this town since I moved here six months ago." She sobered. "I'm sorry about Mr. Young, though. That's bad, but this is like being in a movie."

"A horror movie," Lauren announced from the couch where she settled. "I'm not sure how you can relax when you're a suspect like the rest of us…"

CHAPTER 24

After telling Skylar to knock on the office door when she'd finished cleaning the public areas, Courtney followed Alex and Nathan back to their office. Now they knew the police would be leaving soon, they needed to make their own plans. They settled at the table with their list of suspects.

"As soon as they finish with Braden, go talk to him," Courtney said to Alex, who sat beside her.

"You're kind of getting bossy," Alex said. "You're getting into the role of detective again."

Courtney laughed. "Well, someone has to solve this. You're seeing my administrative skills in action."

"I've already seen your skills while we've gotten this inn up and running in record time, and you already solved one murder." He smiled then leaned over and kissed her.

They'd put in a massive number of hours to accomplish the renovation, and Courtney gloried in the initial setup. "I'm going to follow Skylar around as soon as she's done with the public areas, so I can snoop in the rooms she's cleaning. Maybe I can find something. What are you going to do, Nathan?"

"You aren't ordering him around?" Alex asked.

"He's my older brother. I'm used to him ordering me around."

Nathan smiled at their joking. "I'm checking in with my private detective and giving him the information about the guests. I'm adding Willow to the list as the last person to investigate, in case we missed something with her. Willow definitely has an alibi, but if she planned Phil's death with someone else, an association with one of the other people here might show up. We have to be thorough."

Courtney was glad he didn't add that, because Alex found the body, he remained a suspect to the police. She hoped they'd clear him soon. A knock on the door interrupted her thoughts, and she got up to see who needed them. She opened the door to Braden.

"Can I come in?" He twisted his hands together and hunched his shoulders. "I figure I should come to you, since Alex has wanted to talk to me for the past day."

"Come in."

Alex took the papers they were looking at and stuffed them in her desk drawer. He motioned to Braden to take a chair at the round table where they'd been conferring.

Braden sat down and stared at Alex. "I'm sorry. I don't know how this whole thing got out of hand. I promise you I did not invite everyone here. I told them to stay away, and I don't know who sent the blackmail text to Phil."

Alex folded his hands across his chest. "What I don't understand is why you didn't tell me once it happened."

Braden hung his head and mumbled, "My mom lost a lot of money. I wanted to get it back for her. I knew you wouldn't go along with the plan once they decided to come here."

Alex's lips tightened. "You're right. You should have told the police about the blackmail text. Okay. Start from the beginning and tell us what happened."

"I checked into Mom's accounts and found she paid Phil high prices to invest, and none of the investments were ever lucrative. I gave the information to a friend of mine who is an accountant, and he looked everything over. He told me Mom was swindled."

"Why didn't you come to me?" Alex asked, puzzled. "You know my background."

This time he looked straight at Alex and didn't flinch. "I didn't want to involve you. You are my employer, and I didn't want you to think less of me. I trust you as much as I trust my friend, but I wanted to keep work and my personal life separate. I was moving on after being in jail, and I didn't want to complicate everything. You know—a clean break."

Tears came to Courtney's eyes. Alex's sleepless nights and pacing bothered her because nothing she could do would help him. He'd improved immensely since he returned home from prison for something he hadn't done. Moving to Elm City and starting the inn helped. The residual effects of prison would last much longer than she hoped, and only God could help Alex recover.

Thank goodness Braden had the sense not to involve Alex. Although maybe it would have prevented Phil's death. But here they were now.

"I see." Alex's tone and expression remained calm. "Makes sense."

But Courtney could sense the churning anger under her husband's calm façade. He would feel betrayed since Braden hadn't told them when things changed, and the guests were coming.

"Lauren and I ran into each other outside Phil's house. We were both there for the same reason: for her to get her money back and me to get my mom's money back from Phil. Lauren and I started meeting to discuss what to do. She didn't tell me Phil and Kris were her uncle and aunt.

"Anyway," Braden continued, "I told Lauren Phil's practices were illegal. She told me she would talk to his wife and find out if she knew about Phil's business activities.

"That's when things got out of hand. Kris insisted she didn't know anything and would get the money back to Lauren and my mom. After a month, nothing happened. I stopped my mom from investing with him, and Lauren did the same. But neither one got any money back from Phil, and Kris kept putting Lauren off.

"After the month passed, I took my friend's paperwork about my mom's investments to the police and told them what happened. By then, I had this job. I kept in contact with Detective Zueger and Detective Entz, depending on which one would talk to me, to see what happened. They brought in a forensic accountant to go over Mom's financials.

"Somehow, the investigator found out Rory and Ivy, Melanie's godmother, and Jade's uncle were all scammed. Jade's uncle committed suicide, which brought the investigation to a whole new level. I wasn't kept in the loop any longer. They told me they would work on Mom's case, along with the other clients', and when they had something they could share, they would let us know and told me to wait.

"Somehow, Lauren is the one who found out about Rory, Ivy, Melanie, and Jade. The police weren't the ones to tell her. I guess she found out from Kris. I keep forgetting she's her aunt. Lauren brought us all together a few times to share our stories with each other."

"How did you all end up at Crocus Hill Inn when most of the other guests must live near Minot?" Courtney didn't understand the purpose. "The blackmail supposedly said the person would contact the police, but Phil already knew of the investigation. If Lauren told Kris, then Kris must have told Phil. So why would he come, if he knew the police were already investigating him?"

Braden shook his head, his eyes expressing bewilderment. "Unless Kris didn't tell Phil about our group. Maybe she's the one who sent the text in order to kill him. The others would all come to the inn if Phil came, and there'd be plenty of suspects. I'm sorry I got you involved. I didn't know anything about it until half of the group booked to stay here. By then, it was too late to do anything."

"Too late?" Courtney found her voice rising as Alex's hand reached for hers. "You could have told us everything before they arrived. We would have been prepared. Or, better yet, told them not to come."

"Honey, I know you're upset…" Alex squeezed her hand.

"I told them not to come." Braden's voice shook. "I explained the A New Day program, and told them they'd have to participate. I didn't think they'd want to participate, so they wouldn't come. But they did."

She glared at Braden. "I put my heart into this place. It's been a dream of mine for years. We put a lot of money into it, and now you might have ruined everything. We don't need this kind of notoriety for our opening week. Is anyone going to want to stay here after this?"

"Phil didn't die here." Nathan tried to calm her down. "He died out in the country somewhere."

"You think that's going to make a difference?" she challenged him.

"Let's table it for now." Alex squeezed her hand again, and, this time, she let his touch relax her. The situation wasn't his fault.

Courtney stared at Braden. "So, someone threatened Phil. You all found out, and the others came to stay. You already worked here, which is beside the point."

"That is the point," Nathan corrected her. He studied Braden. "You told people where you worked, and someone took advantage of it."

"Sure. We mentioned our jobs as part of us getting to know each other the few times we got together. We met once a few weeks ago, when I told them not to come here. I couldn't control their actions, and they were determined."

"Which is why they came here," Nathan summed it up. "A pool of suspects in one place. A murderer's dream. Someone enticed Phil here to kill him. They didn't care about the money anymore. They knew he would never give it back. It was premeditated murder."

They sat there in silence as the truth sank in.

"They used Braden like they did us." Alex's shoulders relaxed, and Courtney realized he'd felt betrayed by Braden, but this latest revelation relieved some of the hurt. Although Braden could have told them what the guests planned before they arrived.

"So, we have a cold-blooded murderer to discover." Nathan subdued tone left them with nothing else to say. "That's different."

CHAPTER 25

Alex and Courtney tried to adjust to the fact one of their guests deliberately set up the situation to have multiple suspects, so they could murder Phil and likely get away with it.

A knock on the door made them jump.

Courtney, closest to the door, went to open it. Jade stood there.

"I'm leaving." Jade held out the keycard to her room. "I wanted to give you my keycard and tell you thank you for what you've done for me while I'm here."

Was that irony? Courtney took the card.

"You're welcome. I wish your stay had been for the reason you listed on your registration instead of dealing with Phil." Courtney couldn't think of another way to phrase it.

"Me too. I can't stay any longer because I don't know who killed Phil. Until the police arrest someone, I'm not going to feel safe—here or anywhere. I'm going away to a friend's house, and no one can find me there," Jade said.

"Don't you have to tell the police?" Courtney asked, although it wasn't her problem. But if Jade murdered Phil and disappeared, she didn't want it on her conscience. She didn't want to force Jade to stay until the end of the week either, because any one of them could be in danger.

"Oh, they know. Again, thank you. My luggage is in my car, so I'm ready to go now, except I'll need my gun." Jade stood there waiting.

A sense of foreboding encompassed her at the thought of Jade having her gun back. However, it was her property. "Give me a minute to go get it, and I'll walk you out." She closed the door behind her and left Jade in the hallway, while she went upstairs to her and Alex's safe. She pulled out the gun, handling it carefully, even though she knew it wasn't loaded.

She went downstairs and handed it to Jade, who took it as if it were an extra appendage she was used to holding.

Courtney happily followed Jade out to her vehicle. "Have a safe trip."

Jade thanked her, got into the vehicle, and drove off. Courtney stood there for a minute and then went back inside, hoping the Jade problem was finished.

"So, Jade left." Lauren stated the obvious from her spot on the couch. "I'm considering the same thing as soon as the police get through with my interview this morning. It depends on what Aunt Kris wants to do." She sighed. "She may wait until they are ready to transport Uncle Phil's body back to Minot. I don't know why they took him to Dickinson instead of Minot in the first place."

"Who do you think killed him?" Courtney blurted out. It wasn't what she planned to say.

Lauren shook her head. "I have no idea. It's why I want to leave. That's why Jade left. None of us trust each other anymore. We all started out with the same plan to get our money back, but someone changed the plan, and we don't know who."

"Braden said you were scammed by your uncle?" Phrasing it as a question, she perched on the chair across from Lauren.

"At first I lied to Braden about it being my aunt, and that's what he told the others in the group. The money was an advance for a book I wrote. Uncle Phil promised he would increase the amount with a sound investment. I didn't want anyone to know, but it's all going to come out now. Uncle Phil knew how to take what he wanted." The venom in her voice changed to sadness. "It's not fair. Now Phil is gone, there's no way I'm going to get my money back." Lauren didn't sound like a bereaved niece.

"But won't Kris help you? She's in charge now."

"I wouldn't be surprised if more people came out of the woodwork making claims about Uncle Phil. There won't be enough money to go around to settle, and the police will probably freeze all her assets. And I don't know what Aunt Kris's position is in all this. She may be in legal trouble too." Lauren slumped against the couch.

"Lauren! Lauren!" The cry came from the sunroom, and Lauren jumped up and ran down the hallway.

Courtney followed slowly and saw Lauren reach for Kris as she came out of the room.

"You'll never believe what they're doing." Kris blubbered into a tissue. "They're searching our house in Minot. They have a warrant. I don't know what to do."

Courtney glanced up at Detective Zueger, who stood in the doorway watching the scene.

"Did you call your lawyer?" Lauren asked.

"I don't have one," she wailed. "They're going through all our things, and no one's there to watch them."

"Well, let's get you a lawyer who can check things out. Let's go to my room. My phone's in there, and we can find somebody." She ignored the rest of them and put an arm around her aunt's shoulders.

"What are we going to do?" Kris asked.

"One thing at a time." Lauren pulled Kris into her room and closed the door.

CHAPTER 26

After Lauren hustled Kris to her room, Courtney stared at Detective Zueger as they stood in the hallway. "You're looking for proof he scammed his clients."

"No comment."

She grinned. "I have several guests who have told me what's going on, and you have too many suspects."

"We've narrowed it down." He smirked.

"Is Alex off the list?"

"Yes. You, Alex, and both Dr. Alois and Hugh Alois are off the list."

Her knees weakened in relief.

"Now I've let you know, I'd like to talk to Skylar. She and I haven't talked yet."

Courtney couldn't imagine Skylar shooting anyone, but she had also believed in Braden at one point.

"Call it covering all the bases."

"Okay. I hear the vacuum upstairs. I'll get her." She stepped over to the side door in the hallway leading upstairs to their apartment. On her way upstairs, she thanked God she and Alex were no longer suspects. She hadn't realized how heavy it weighed on her mind.

Skylar's back was toward her when she opened the door into the hallway. She knocked on the wall to get her attention. When Skylar didn't turn around, she saw something in one of her ears. Skylar was listening to something while she cleaned.

When Courtney touched her lightly on the arm, Skylar jumped and turned around. She shut off the vacuum and grinned. "Hi, Boss. What can I do for you?"

"It's not me. The police are downstairs waiting in the sunroom for you. They want to ask you a few questions."

Skylar's face paled, and she licked her lips. "Why me? I didn't know the man who died. Well, except for a few minutes' conversation."

"They need to talk to everyone involved in the scam. Your uncle died. I'm sure it's a formality and nothing important." She hoped, anyway.

"Can you go with me?" Skylar's hand gripped the handle of the vacuum.

"If you want me to." Excitement coursed through her. She wanted to hear what they asked Skylar and if they'd made progress in the investigation. This was her opportunity.

"I do."

They walked down the stairs in silence, and Courtney followed Skylar into the sunroom.

"Mrs. Richmond, I didn't expect you." Detective Zueger squinted at her.

"I want her here," Skylar jumped in. "I won't answer any questions unless she's here."

"If you insist, I can't stop her from being here. Maybe it's better if Mrs. Richmond knows what we found," the sheriff said. "Obviously, when you're back in Minot, there won't be any more civilian involvement in the investigation. A warning for you, Mrs. Richmond. You won't be welcome to sit with anyone. They can find a lawyer."

"Got it." She tried to sound agreeable, surprised at how often he'd let her in on the interviews. She nodded at Detective Entz, who sat at the far end of the table.

"We will be taping this interview. Do you have any objection?" Sheriff Warren asked Skylar.

She glanced at Courtney, who shrugged. "I guess not," Skylar said.

"Okay." The sheriff started the recording and stated the preliminaries: those present, the date and time. "Full name Skylar Kittrell. You have two children, two and four years old. Who are they with right now?"

"My mother babysits them when I'm working. We live together." Skylar stared down at the table.

"And your husband? What does he do?"

"I'm not married." Her face flamed, and she stared at him as if daring him to judge her. Her shoe tapped on the floor as she jiggled her foot.

"Where were you between 1:00 p.m. and 6:00 p.m. Monday?" Sheriff Warren asked her.

"Home, baking cookies with Mom and the kids."

"Did anyone other than your mom see you there during those hours?"

She sat quietly for a few minutes, except for a slight twirl of her fingers. "I don't remember anyone stopping by the house in the afternoon. I imagine some of the older neighbors might have seen my car in her driveway, but I'm not sure."

"We'll check with them. Anything else you can remember about the times you were here at the inn when the other guests were present? Anything stand out in your mind about any of them?"

"They whispered a lot when they thought no one paid attention. I couldn't hear what they said, but Braden and Lauren had what seemed like a deep conversation."

"What made you believe it mattered so much to them?"

She hesitated. "I've seen them when our group got together to discuss how to get our money back from Phil. Sometimes, the rest of us felt like they planned things we didn't know about until later. Their expressions were serious, like it was a big deal." Her foot started tapping again.

"Anything else?" he asked.

"Rory and Ivy appear to be on their honeymoon, but I've seen their expressions when they didn't believe anyone was watching. They looked worried. I suppose it has to do with the money they lost to Mr. Young."

"You know they lost money?"

"They told us in Minot." The tapping stopped.

Courtney held back her annoyance Skylar knew about the situation with Phil. More betrayal.

"And you say you didn't know him before he came here?" His measured stare brought a lump to Courtney's throat. Something was coming.

The shoe tapping started up again. "No. I never met him until he was a guest here. He'd scammed my Uncle Hank, but I only talked about him to Jade, and she told me about this group."

Courtney thought she was telling the truth.

"You heard his name though?" he repeated the question.

Courtney braced herself for whatever came next.

Skylar's gaze fell to the table again. "As I said, I heard his name. I guess you know my uncle committed suicide." She glanced over at Courtney and let go of her arm.

The sheriff looked over at Courtney. "I take it you didn't know your housekeeper was in on the plan too?"

"Not until Phil's death," she murmured. If she opened her mouth farther, she'd scream at Skylar.

"There was no plan." Skylar shook her head. "I already worked here when we heard about the text. Braden and Lauren were going to approach Kris to get the money back. When Phil refused Kris's pleas, Braden went to the police. You and you." She pointed to the Minot detectives. "That's when things got out of control."

"You're blaming us?"

Courtney couldn't read the detective's expression but caught an underlying hint of incredulity in his voice.

"None of us were going to come to the inn until you refused to do anything." Skylar's defiance concluded with more shoe tapping.

"I don't remember refusing to help you. I believe I told Braden and Lauren I would investigate," the detective stared at her.

His expression would have caused Courtney to wilt—but not Skylar.

"Why did it take so long? You're getting a search warrant because Phil died. Why not last week before everyone arrived here? You could have stopped this whole charade." Skylar scolded him as if he were her four-year-old.

Skylar's sudden backbone showed. Her earlier anxiety had disappeared, replaced by a lack of fear, even though she remained a suspect.

CHAPTER 27

"We couldn't jump into getting a search warrant for Mr. Young's paperwork," Detective Zueger informed Courtney and Skylar. "We need proof of wrongdoing before we get a warrant."

"You had Braden's mom's paperwork and Lauren's paperwork for three months. I don't see why it took so long. There's been plenty of time to look at a few papers and see if something's wrong. If Braden's accountant can find a problem in a few days, your resources could do it faster. Or at least in the same amount of time." No hesitation. No shoe tapping. And no red face. She was perfectly composed.

A shiver ran across Courtney's neck at Skylar's collected demeanor. How had she misread Skylar's personality?

"You've been in Elm City for approximately six months, correct?" Detective Zueger ignored her accusation.

"Yes. About that long."

"Did you come because you wanted to be here when Phil Young came, and you wanted to pretend you didn't know him or anything about what was going on?"

"Of course not. As far as I knew, Phil only planned on coming two weeks ago. Per what Braden told me."

More tapping, and it started to get on Courtney's nerves.

"Besides, my mother lives here and has for years. I needed someone to babysit. When Braden told me he worked here, I hoped I might be able to get a job. It worked out. Courtney and Alex hired me about a month ago."

Detective Zueger's gaze swung Courtney's way. "Is that the timeframe you remember?"

"We did hire her about a month ago. I met her mother, Lucy, in the grocery store, and she asked me if we were hiring any help. I mentioned we needed a cook and a housekeeper. She said her daughter was looking for work and had experience. Her references checked out."

A smug look crossed Skylar's face. "I told you."

"You did." He didn't look convinced she wasn't involved in the plot though. "Anything else you want to add?"

"There's no way Jade could have killed him. I know she's high on the suspect list, but we heard about her approaching Phil. She couldn't pull the trigger. If she couldn't do it then, there's no way she could have done it later. She gets angry, tells someone off, and then she's over it. Plus, Courtney and Alex have her gun. I was there when they took it."

"Okay. We'll keep it in mind." He glanced at the sheriff.

"Interview over, 11:30 a.m." Sheriff Warren clicked off the recorder and told them they could go.

"Would you mind asking Rory to come back here?" Sheriff Warren asked Courtney.

She got up to follow Skylar out of the room, but the sheriff called her back.

He waited until the door closed behind Skylar. "We're going to serve a search warrant on Kris and Phil Young's room. Detective Zueger and Detective Entz will oversee the search, so they'll be waiting by the front door for the warrant. The server should be here shortly."

Just what they needed. What a circus. Courtney's eye twitched, and she took a step toward the table where they sat. "A warrant? Do you always do that?"

"In this case, yes. Guns, embezzling. Lots of accusations being thrown around, along with the Minot detectives' investigation."

"Thanks for letting me know." She left them and entered the hallway, letting the door slam behind her.

Lauren and Kris came out of Lauren's room.

"I have an attorney meeting the police searching our house." Kris bleakly shared before she headed toward her own room. "I'm going to lie down—there's nothing more I can do," she added with a twist of her lips.

"I can't let you go back to your room, Mrs. Young," Detective Zueger told her. "Detective Entz will be guarding the room until the search warrant has been served."

"You have a search warrant for my room?" Her shoulders sagged, and Courtney was relieved Lauren stood by to catch her aunt.

"Let's go back to my room." Lauren took her aunt's arm. "We'll prop the door open, and you'll know when they're here. You can stand and watch them from the hallway if you want. I'll be with you. We don't have time to find another lawyer." She threw a scathing look at the detectives.

With the fight knocked out of her, she followed Lauren, who propped her room door open with one of the chairs and sat there.

"Can I get you something?" Courtney asked her. Maybe Kris had something to do with Phil's death, but if she didn't, she was a grieving widow. "Maybe some tea?"

"Chamomile, if you have it." She lay on Lauren's bed with her arm across her eyes.

"I'll take a soda and a helping of whatever's for lunch today," Lauren told her.

"Sure."

Skylar went to get the food and drink before helping Willow get the noon meal on the table. Courtney tried to hide her anger over another employee betraying them. Venting to Nathan and Alex would relieve some of the pressure building inside her.

The others stood in the hallway while she went to the office to find out what they were doing. They should have been done with Braden a while ago.

On her way, she went through the list of guests in her head. She couldn't picture anyone killing Phil. Skylar surprised her, and she'd been in Elm City all afternoon. Definitely on the list. Jade's erratic behavior earlier in the day put her in the running too. Maybe they'd done it together. Their uncle's death devastated both of them.

She couldn't leave out Lauren and Kris either. Lauren's uncle betrayed her. And Kris was the wife. Wasn't the wife always a suspect? Maybe she'd tired of Phil's scams. Since Kris was Lauren's father's sister, the suspicion focused on Kris must annoy Lauren.

There were too many options, and she hoped the police had some idea by now. Which made her think of the gun. Surely they could trace the serial number on the gun. She needed to ask Nathan.

CHAPTER 28

Opening the office door, Courtney took a step back, surprised to see Alex and Nathan talking to Rory and Ivy. She felt cheated because she wanted to talk to her guests. So far, she hadn't had time to search rooms or talk to anyone except Lauren and listen in on Skylar's interview with the police.

Rory and Ivy got up quickly from the table where they sat with Nathan and Alex. She got the feeling they wanted to escape the office.

She told them the sheriff wanted them in the enclosed sunroom and quickly closed the office door behind them. "Anything of interest from them?"

"Nothing new," Alex said. "They told us basically what Kris said. They met Phil at the shooting range. Kris wanted to leave, so Phil took her to Elm City and dropped her off to sightsee. Then Phil came back to the shooting range. He left before they did. They could have followed him."

"They don't have an alibi?" Courtney asked, sitting down at the table.

"No. What's going on out there?" Alex asked.

"They've executed a search warrant for Kris's room. They're in there now. Nathan, why don't you go out there and make sure they don't search the rest of the inn without the proper paperwork?" Courtney knew just how to get rid of Nathan so she could see Alex alone.

Nathan rose from his chair and hurried out of the door in an instant.

When it closed behind him, Courtney turned to Alex. "I'm going to run a quick errand in Elm City. Why don't you join the group out there and get our guests to the table for lunch? I want to be back here before the police leave for the day. They did say they weren't returning this afternoon."

"What do you have planned?" Alex frowned. "I don't want you running around alone when we don't know what's going on."

"I'm safer in my vehicle and driving away than staying here. I'm going to visit Mrs. B, who lives across from Skylar. I want an opinion on Skylar, since I misread her character. I must go now. One piece of information for you to mull over before I return: Skylar and Jade aren't cousins, but Hank was their uncle on different sides of the family. He committed suicide."

"What?"

"Yes. Now, I'm going to peek into Jade's room and see if she forgot anything when she left, and Skylar can clean in there when she's done with lunch. As for you, how about watching our guests for a while?"

She patted him on the arm and urged him out of the office. "Your time with Nathan has been superseded by his interest in what's going on out there." She waved toward the hallway. "I'm sure you'll enjoy everything happening while gathering

the guests." She smiled. "I found out we aren't
suspects any longer, so try to relax."

"Good news." He exhaled fully and laughed
at her devious plotting. "Sure. I understand, Boss.
I'm on eavesdropping duty."

"Don't you forget it." She walked along the
hall, past the police and other guests who lingered
in the hallway, watching what happened with Kris's
room. She saw Alex grimace as he joined Nathan.

After opening Jade's room door with her
master keycard, she stepped inside. The door swung
shut behind her without latching. She went into the
bathroom first, looking for items Jade might have
left. There weren't any toiletries lying around. She
swiftly opened the vanity's drawers. Nothing.

She walked around the room, searching the
windowsill, the desk, the desk drawers. Nothing. So
far, the place looked ready for Skylar to clean.

She did one last thing: peeked under the bed.
Sometimes people accidentally kicked articles of
clothing under the bed when they packed. What she
found was a shoebox. Nothing else.

She slid her hand under the bed and pulled
the shoebox toward her, curious what kind of shoes
Jade thought she needed that couldn't be packed in
a suitcase. Maybe a pair of heels for going out at
night? Courtney opened the box, and her mouth
dropped open.

A gun. She had taken Jade's keycard and
returned Jade's gun. Who left this one here? And
why? The gun used to kill Phil was left with his
body.

Courtney sat back on her heels and stared. She wouldn't touch the gun or the box again. Had someone come into the room after Jade left and slid the gun under the bed, so they wouldn't have a gun found in their possession? There were too many guns around—she didn't know what to believe.

CHAPTER 29

Courtney left the box with the gun on the floor and went out to find Sheriff Warren, since the murder was his case. He appeared unwilling to leave the group, but she convinced him it would only take a few minutes.

He walked the few steps down the hall to Jade's room, and Courtney used her keycard again. She pointed to the shoebox with the gun inside. "I found this under Jade's bed as I did a last run-through of the room before Skylar cleans."

"Give me a minute." He walked around the room, inspecting it, much like she had, albeit with a more experienced eye. Satisfied there was nothing more to see, he walked over to the box and looked down at the contents. "This is unusual."

"So, whose gun is this? Alex and I put Jade's gun in our safe upstairs. Alex told me the weapon used to kill Phil was found at the scene." Courtney didn't frame it as a question.

The sheriff's gaze rose to hers, and she cringed at his blue glare. "Keep that information to yourself, please."

"I will."

"Did you touch it?" He pointed at the gun and shoebox.

"Only the box and lid when I pulled it from under the bed. Once I lifted the lid, I put it on the floor and didn't touch anything else. Especially not the gun."

"Okay. We're going to leave it here for now. As soon as the techs are done with Kris's room, I'll have them come in and look around, take pictures, and gather evidence. Do I have your permission to search this room before the techs come in and permission for the techs to gather information?"

"You do. But only this room," she warned him. "I have to run an errand in Elm City. Ask Alex for the keycard to get into the room when you're ready. Nathan will probably have a form for you to sign."

He agreed.

She went down the hallway and pulled Alex and Nathan into the sunroom. "New plan. I found a gun in Jade's room."

As they both opened their mouths to say something, she stopped them. "I need to run to Elm City. Make sure no one goes into Jade's room until the police are done in there. I gave them permission to search the room. But only that room." She gave Nathan a pointed look. "Sorry it goes against your lawyerly instincts not to have a search warrant. Sheriff Warren will ask you for the keycard when he's ready, Alex. Nathan, you can ensure the detectives don't overstep and have them sign something if you want."

"Okay." Alex gave her a quick hug. "Things are happening now, aren't they?"

She was happy he wasn't shaking anymore. He looked calmer since Nathan arrived and learning they weren't suspects any longer. "Yes, they are.

Let's hope they find the murderer soon, and we can get back to normal around here. I have to run."

He let her go, and she stepped away with a swift wave. "Go watch over everything."

She knew Nathan lived for moments like this. Alex, not so much.

The trip into Elm City passed quickly as her thoughts went over the morning events. Alex was right. Things were moving, and a lot happened in a few days. Lauren and Kris were related. Jade and Skylar were related.

All those people had money stolen. The police were constantly around. Nothing went as planned for their opening. They'd given up on any sessions for the week, except appointments with Clarissa and specific requests with Hugh. This group hadn't come to reset their lives.

She wanted to talk alone with Nathan and Alex. They'd been passing each other coming and going and not having any in-depth conversation except the suspect lists. Nothing but brief updates. They said nothing came from their discussion with Rory and Ivy, but those two were the last to see Phil alive. That usually meant something. Or maybe she'd read too many mysteries.

They'd been in there a long time and discovered nothing? At least she'd been there long enough to catch most of Braden's story. After everything was cleared up about Phil, they were going to have to decide what to do about Braden and Skylar. As soon as everyone planned to stay at the inn, they should have informed her and Alex.

She suddenly thought of Melanie. She hadn't been around all morning. Courtney tried to remember if her vehicle had been in the parking lot.

When was the last time she'd seen Melanie? At breakfast. Did she leave the inn until the police left? They said they were leaving around noon, as soon as they finished a few things.

A few things, such as a warrant to search Kris's room. And now a search of Jade's room.

Which brought her right back to the question bothering her. Whose gun was used to kill Phil? And had the police already found the owner by the serial number on it? They might even have a good idea of the murderer's identity. Information they wouldn't share with her or Alex.

CHAPTER 30

Courtney reached Elm City in about ten minutes and drove directly to Skylar's house. She needed to get back to the inn as soon as possible. Skylar lived with her mother, Lucy, and Courtney hoped Lucy was home.

After a brief wait, Lucy answered the door. "Well, Courtney. This is a surprise. Come in."

Lucy led her into the living room. The open room held a faded blue plaid sofa and curtains, surrounded by a plentiful gathering of figurines on shelves, and two comfortable padded blue armchairs. A scratched rectangular coffee table rounded out the furnishings.

Two children she assumed were Skylar's kids sat on the floor at the coffee table and colored. Courtney smiled at them, and they smiled shyly back at her. Neither appeared afraid of her. She thought maybe the two-year-old would run to her grandmother, but they seemed content with her in the room.

"Have a chair," Lucy suggested, pointing to the armchair farthest away from the coffee table. "Can I get you something to drink? Water, lemonade, soda, or coffee?"

"No, thank you." Courtney perched on the edge of the chair.

Lucy took this as a sign she could sit too and settled on the sofa directly across from Courtney. "How can I help you?"

"I'm going to jump right in since I don't have much time, and I'm sure you're busy with the children." She glanced at them. She'd have to speak in general terms because, while the four-year-old didn't seem to be listening, she knew better. Children heard when you didn't think they did. "I'm sure Skylar told you what's been going on at work."

Lucy clasped her hands together. "She sure did. I was glad she was here yesterday baking cookies all afternoon with us. I don't want her mixed up in anything. I'm scared for her."

She did look frightened and pale. Her eyes fluttered back and forth between Courtney and the children.

"She didn't leave at all?" Courtney asked.

"No. The children needed her, and we don't always get to spend much time together now she's busier. It was a nice afternoon," Lucy said.

"We had chocolate chip cookies," the little boy said. He looked up at her with his big brown eyes. "I'm four years old."

"You're a big boy," Courtney said, leaning forward to be at his level. "What's your name?"

"Kyle. Her name is Violet." He pointed at the little girl. "She's named after a flower."

"They're both nice names." A slight tug at her heart came at the thought she and Alex might have a few children someday.

"Thank you," Kyle said politely. "We had to wait for our cookies until after our nap though."

"Sometimes we have to wait for good things," Courtney said.

"That's what Grandma told me. She ran out of chocolate chips and went to the store." He went back to coloring.

Lucy laughed. "I can't keep enough food in the house since they moved here. I'm learning what they'll eat and what they won't."

"Well, from what I understand, that changes from day to day."

"For sure."

Courtney stood up. "I wanted to let you know we're looking out for your daughter while she's with us and will do what we can to protect her."

Lucy stood too. "Thank you. It's hard not to feel protective of your children no matter their age."

They walked to the hallway, and Courtney made sure the children hadn't followed them. She stepped out onto the front steps and held open the screen door. "Was Hank your brother?"

Lucy started, and her face paled. "No. He was my husband's last remaining sibling. My husband left years ago, and I thought we'd have a lot more years with Hank. He was everything to Skylar. Such a caring, sensitive man. I'm not surprised he did what he did." She glanced behind her. "It caused a lot of pain in his extended family."

"I'm sorry," Courtney said. "I know it doesn't help, but I am."

"Well, I'm not sorry for what happened to Phil, but those young people getting together was misguided." She shook her head. "I almost hope they don't find the guilty party."

Courtney nodded and said goodbye to her, thinking about Phil having a lot of enemies as she went down the sidewalk to her car. Not only the group who stayed at her inn. She hoped the sheriff took it all into account.

At least the detective finally got a search warrant to get all of Phil Young's paperwork, and hopefully something would point to the person who sent Phil the text to be at the inn. She didn't want the guilty person to be one of the young people who tried to make the situation right, even though they'd gone about it all wrong.

The thought of the gun at the scene of Phil's death popped into her mind as she buckled up and drove back to the inn. An unknown gun could point to an outsider. How long did it take to search a gun's serial number for ownership? She'd check online when she had a minute. Or ask Nathan.

CHAPTER 31

Courtney entered through the front door of the inn. Everyone except law enforcement sat at the dining table finishing lunch. Alex smiled at her from his end of the table.

When she sat down in the chair next to him, he said, "The police are in the sunroom. The detectives and sheriff say they have one more interview, and then they're leaving."

"Thank goodness," Lauren said. "Having my space invaded is not my idea of how to write a book."

"Did you come here to write?" Courtney asked but then regretted her sarcastic tone.

There were lots of startled glances at her from the others at the table.

"I hoped to get some writing time in," Lauren responded evenly and returned Courtney's look with a complacent one of her own.

Courtney didn't respond.

"The detectives are in Jade's room right now, and then they'll do the interview with you," Alex said.

She didn't appreciate him mentioning it in front of their guests. On the other hand, what difference did it make? They'd all know as soon as she was called back to the "interview room."

"Great." Still too angry at her guests to be nervous, she dished up a plate of food and joined Alex at the head of the table. She finished her food in record time and looked around the table.

"Anyone else planning on checking out today?"

Everyone shook their heads.

"Okay. Don't forget your appointment with Dr. Alois. It's required even if you only sit there."

They nodded agreeably, and all seemed to be in a good mood. Melanie was at the table, so Courtney could quit worrying about her. She did want to talk to her though—after the police left. Right now, she needed to let Willow and Skylar know their duties for the rest of the day.

"I'm going to the kitchen," she told Alex. "Why don't you and Nathan join me for a couple of minutes?"

Both men got up from the table while everyone watched them, no doubt wondering what was going on now.

When she passed Jade's room on the way to see Willow in the kitchen, she ignored the activity. She knew what they were doing. She was more interested in talking to Alex.

When they entered the sitting room area of the big kitchen, Courtney explained to Nathan she needed an hour to talk with Alex. Stressed and missing her husband, she wanted time to discuss the past day with him. She couldn't believe Phil's death had only happened yesterday. Today felt more like Friday instead of Tuesday.

"Alex and I are going upstairs to confer. You get to be in charge," she told Nathan, smiling at him. "Right up your alley."

He winked back. "You're right. Nothing I like doing more than directing murderers and suspects."

"If you need something, ask Willow or Braden for help. If they don't know, text one of us."

With that out of the way, she trudged to the dining room table in the great room and told the guests Nathan was their contact person for the next hour if they needed anything. Then she followed Alex down the hallway and up the staircase to their apartment.

She dropped onto the black-and-white checkered couch, and Alex sat down beside her.

"Hi," he said. "What a marathon run, managing everyone."

She laughed. "Did I sound like a drill sergeant ordering the troops? Because that's what I felt like. And it was wonderful being in control. I haven't had you alone since last night, but I was asleep when you came to bed, and we hardly talked this morning before I left the room."

"Two ships, et cetera."

"Exactly. Not liking this start to our inn." She twined her fingers with his and wiggled a little on the couch. Then she pulled the pillow tucked in the corner out from under her. A cute black stuffed animal, a terrier, beguiled her when she saw it in the store. She set it on her lap with her free hand.

"It's not exactly been the best start to our opening," Alex agreed.

"And the police are going to ask me more questions before they leave." She held back a sigh.

"Take Nathan with you. I'll hold down the fort with the guests. And then, hopefully, the sheriff will leave us alone and call suspects into his office. The detective will stay in Minot and continue investigating Phil's money matters."

"Right." She leaned her head on his shoulder. "Are you going to be mad at me if I tell you I'm already investigating the murder myself?"

He laughed. "No. After you wrote out those suspect lists, I knew you were going to be scavenging around until you figured out who killed Phil."

"Glad you're easy-going about it." She squeezed his hand.

"I wouldn't exactly put it that way. I don't like you being in danger. Speaking of which, what did you go to Elm City for?"

She lifted her head and moved slightly away to see his face. "I stopped by Skylar's house. Ever since I found out Skylar and Jade are cousins, I've wondered if maybe we have a team of killers. The previous case we solved when renovating the inn involved more than one person. There's Lauren and Kris, who are related to Phil. Rory and Ivy lost money. There's Jade and Skylar, who are related to their Uncle Hank."

"The one who committed suicide."

"Right. I talked to Skylar's mom to assure her we are watching out for her daughter."

"And you were there to ask her questions too," Alex said.

"Yes. I wanted to check on Skylar's alibi."

"And what did you find out?"

"I found out Skylar's mother wasn't at the house every moment Skylar was. However, I don't see how Skylar could have left when her mother ran to the grocery store for an item or two. Someone needed to watch Skylar's two kids. Neighbors will be interviewed by the police, and I have no doubt Skylar's car stayed in the driveway the whole afternoon.

"Who do you think killed Phil?" she asked him.

CHAPTER 32

"I have no idea who killed him, but I brought this upstairs with me." Alex moved away from Courtney on the couch and pulled three sheets of paper out of his back pocket. "Thought we might want to add more items to your list of suspects." He set the papers on the coffee table and spread them out.

Courtney got up and went to the kitchen area to get a pen. Their apartment had an open floor plan for the kitchen, dining, and living room area. Two bedrooms and two bathrooms sat at the east end of the top floor.

"I've been dying to ask what Rory and Ivy said to you and Nathan," she said on her way back to the couch. She leaned forward and pulled the papers toward her. Then she clicked the pen and added notes to the lists.

On the "Clear" page, she added Alex being cleared and Clarissa's alibi.

Alex – no motive and questionable alibi. Alibi confirmed.

Courtney – alibi and no motive

Nathan – no known motive

Clarissa – no motive and possible alibi (Check for sure to get the police's attention away from her.) Alibi confirmed.

Hugh – alibi and no motive

Willow – alibi (Check for sure, but busy and vehicle didn't leave parking lot.)

"Braden had an alibi. I don't know why I didn't think of it sooner. Remember, he was digging in the yard and here until he went to pick up Kris? Phil was already dead by then."

They smiled at each other. "Thank goodness it's not Braden," Alex said before his smile disappeared. "Unless he planned it with someone else."

"I'm adding him to the cleared list. I don't believe he did it."

"Agreed," Alex said.

She added a few names of those cleared:
Braden – motive (mother lost money) and opportunity when he picked up Kris. Note: Alibi now confirmed. Phil was killed while Braden was working at the inn.

Melanie – motive (godmother lost money) and opportunity. Note: with Clarissa during murder.

She crumpled up the list that said "Possible," on which she'd written:
Skylar – no idea about motive, but not at work, possible opportunity.

They didn't need the list any longer since Skylar would be added to the "Definite Suspect" list.

On the "Definite Suspect" list, she added notes on Skylar, Kris, Ivy, and Rory:

Kris – motive (money and reputation?) and opportunity. Last known person to see Phil alive besides Rory and Ivy.

Lauren – motive (lost money) and opportunity, Phil's niece.

Jade – motive (Uncle Hank death), opportunity and gun. (Does she have another gun? Hers wasn't used.)

Rory – motive (lost money, asked for refund, must be desperate for funds) and opportunity. Last to see Phil alive aside from Kris and Ivy.

Ivy – motive (lost money, must be desperate for funds), opportunity, and last to see Phil alive aside from Kris and Rory.

Added:

Skylar – motive (Uncle Hank death), questionable opportunity, firm alibi from mother??

She passed the two lists back to Alex to study. "So, tell me about Rory and Ivy. I haven't said much more to them than our initial greeting and refusing Rory's refund request."

"He asked me again, more insistently," Alex said as he set the papers on his lap. They settled back on the couch again. "I asked Nathan what we needed to do, and he suggested we wait until the police arrest someone and then decide about refunds."

"Makes sense. I don't want to refund a murderer." She shivered. She couldn't believe a guest downstairs killed someone.

"They didn't have much news to tell us. Their dream of home ownership died when they lost the downpayment on a house, unless Kris returned their money. Getting any money back is unlikely. I'm sure the detective found a way to freeze assets, if they have any evidence.

"The police confirmed Phil took Kris to Elm City at the time they specified. You'll be happy to know I called the gun range and double-checked." He hid his face from her.

She leaned toward him and, putting her hand on his cheek, turned his face to hers. "Are you investigating too?"

He nodded. His brown eyes held a gleam in them.

"Aha." She grinned. "You're having fun."

He grimaced. "Well, in a way. Now I'm cleared. I mean, it's intriguing—'fun' seems like the wrong word to use."

She shook her head. "You and Nathan, I see. He can pull anyone into his enthusiasms. Don't worry. I know the actual death isn't fun, and being a suspect isn't fun. Trying to figure out who did it is certainly a change of pace from choosing floorings and dealing with construction workers."

"We haven't worked with our A New Day program participants though." He sounded sad.

"Now, don't go there, Alex. They came for a purpose, and it wasn't to improve themselves or make big decisions, like we meant this place to be.

Although *someone* made a big decision, I'm writing this week off as far as the program goes. Who knows, maybe it did benefit someone, and I don't mean the murderer. Besides, they're all seeing Clarissa this afternoon. Maybe she can help some of the innocent ones come to terms with everything happening."

"You're right, as usual."

"I'm concerned about how this affects the business, which makes me feel cold and heartless when somebody is dead."

"I know." He squeezed her shoulders in a hug. "It's human to be concerned. Unfortunately, we're going to have to wait and see how many reservations we have after this week. At least we have two weeks because of Paul's wedding before we were going to have any more guests."

"You're right. We'll see where we stand with the business after the wedding." Of course, she'd be watching for reservations in the next two weeks. "Phil needed to be stopped but not murdered. I wish the detective had done the search warrant at Phil's Minot house last week, and this whole week wouldn't have happened. They might have arrested him before everyone came."

Courtney hugged him. "But here we are. We've gotten to practice the cooking, cleaning, and logistics for our next guests: your family. We may be trying to find out who killed Phil, but let's remember we're celebrating a wedding in a few weeks. Our current guests will be gone soon, and they won't be our problem anymore. Unfortunately, we don't know what the consequences will be for further bookings. Guests may not want to stay here after what's happened."

"You're right." He kissed the top of her head where it rested on his shoulder. "Until then, we investigate."

She smiled sadly and sat up. "Maybe we'll have to start a different business."

"Let's worry about damage control after this week." He patted her shoulder.

She kissed his cheek. "You're right. Let's concentrate on the investigation. We've crumpled those two sheets on your lap. Let's take a look again."

"Let's talk about Jade. Who put the gun under her bed? I doubt she left a second one behind. Once we took the first one from her, she wouldn't want to bring another one into the building. If she had another one, she would have left it in her vehicle," Alex said.

Courtney sighed. "I like Jade. I don't want it to be her. And she seemed genuinely upset and scared when she left this morning."

"I feel like whatever happened with the gun is a big clue. I mean, if Jade didn't leave it, who got into her room? We've ruled out Willow. She doesn't appear involved in any of this. Which leaves Braden and Skylar who have access to Jade's room. Discounting us and Hugh and Clarissa, of course. Braden wouldn't help her. I'm sure of it. He didn't tell us about the guests' real agenda. I think he learned his lesson after what happened to Phil and would tell us if something concerning the inn happened again. Am I being naïve?"

Alex nodded. "I agree with you, but we don't know."

"Right. Of our suspects, Rory, Ivy, Lauren, and Kris don't have access to the room, as far as we know. Unless one of them can hack codes. But there was a lot of coming and going in the hallway, and it would have been obvious if anyone went into the room. That leaves Skylar. Why would she leave a gun in Jade's room? The gun wasn't the murder weapon, so why would anyone care?"

"Let's put the question on the back burner. I have no idea."

"Me either," Courtney agreed. "The only other idea I have, is someone put it there before Jade left. They distracted her, got into her room, and left it there."

"Because they wanted it out of their room. Once we'd discovered Jade's gun, they didn't want us to find theirs because they had the idea to kill Phil. But they didn't use the gun. Did they change their mind? Or use a different gun and left this one behind to confuse everyone? They counted on Jade not looking under her bed because she didn't have anything else there."

"That we know of, anyway. Maybe she saw the box and left it there, knowing it had nothing to do with her. If she brought up its presence, she'd be stuck explaining something she didn't understand. Who knows?" Courtney rubbed her neck. "I can't figure this out right now. How about you?"

"Nope. Back-burner it."

Courtney got up and paced in front of the couch. "Have we gotten anywhere with our talk?"

She stopped pacing and stood by the coffee table, looking down at the two papers lying there. "We have Braden and Skylar because they have access anytime, if they planned it with someone else. For duos, we have Rory and Ivy, or Kris and Lauren, or Skylar and Jade. Which only excludes Melanie, if that's the case." She sighed. "Only one person off the suspect list."

Courtney continued pacing. "I believe we can take Kris off the list for shooting Phil. She has an alibi. The possibility of her being seen if someone picked her up again once Phil dropped her off is substantial. Small towns have eyes everywhere."

Alex nodded. "She had no way to get back out to where I found him without someone seeing her. Would she take the chance? Okay. We've already crossed off Melanie, and Kris could have planned something with Lauren. What about Lauren?"

"She's angry enough," Courtney said. "She seems like someone who could plan it. Her alibi is slim."

Courtney's expression mirrored his. "Are we getting anywhere?"

"No. How are we going to get proof on someone?" Alex asked.

"Question them all," Courtney answered.

CHAPTER 33

Alex shook his head at Courtney. "You are not going to question them all. It's not safe."

She glared at him. "Of course I am. We need to know the answer, and we only have a few days before they're gone. In fact, they can leave any time they want. I wouldn't be surprised if we woke up tomorrow, and a few more of the guests have their bags packed."

"Well, it won't be Rory and Ivy. They're going to get their money's worth. Kris is waiting for them to release Phil's body, and she doesn't want to return to the mess in Minot yet. Plus, she's got Lauren here to semi-comfort her."

"And Lauren won't desert her aunt. At least I don't think she will," Courtney added. "We're left with Melanie, who we've eliminated as a suspect. If she leaves, I wouldn't blame her."

Her phone buzzed with a text. She pulled her phone out of her jeans pocket and looked at the message. "It's Nathan. The police are ready for my final interview. Can't wait to get this over with and have them leave."

"I kind of liked having them around as protection for our guests and us." Alex pulled his own phone out of his pocket and sent a quick message. "Nathan will meet you down at the sunroom door. I'm going down to see to our guests while you two are with the police."

They walked down the stairs and, at the bottom, opened the door into the hallway right by the sunroom door. Nathan stood there waiting for her.

"How's it going out there with our guests?" Alex asked.

"Nothing happening. All quiet," Nathan reported.

"Great. Take care of my girl." Alex kissed Courtney on the cheek and walked down the hall away from them.

Courtney felt a twinge of loss, but her big brother, Nathan the lawyer, would protect her.

Nathan laughed. "He's not going anywhere."

She punched him on the arm before she opened the door. Only Sheriff Warren remained. The detectives must have gone back to Minot after finishing the search of Kris's and Jade's rooms.

She took a seat at the end of the table, and Nathan sat beside her. The sheriff sat across from them, paging through the notebook in front of him.

"Thanks for joining me," Sheriff Warren said politely.

"You're welcome." Might as well start on a pleasant note.

"I have a few questions, and then I'll be leaving." He picked up his notebook. "I want to confirm Skylar's movements for yesterday. I know you were in here when she talked with us, but I wanted to know if you thought of anything later?"

She shook her head. "She worked and then left for the day. I don't remember the exact time." It was only yesterday. How could she not remember?

"Give me a minute." She wished Alex were there, so she could ask him. "She ate lunch with us. She cleared the dishes and carted them into Willow's area. Then she left. It must have been around 1:00 p.m. I'm not positive though. I didn't check the time."

"Close enough. How about Willow? She says she stayed in the kitchen and only stopped for a nap mid-afternoon on the recliner in the sitting room by the kitchen area."

"Sounds right. It was her first full day cooking and dealing with our guests; she wouldn't have time to go anywhere. Every time I went by, I heard her working in the kitchen, and I did see her napping in the afternoon.

"I don't know the time she slept. It had to be between when Skylar left at about 1:00 p.m. and Braden getting a snack around the time Kris called about Phil missing. Braden talked to her then, because he went into the kitchen where she was working."

"Okay. Sounds clear. Was Braden gone at all?" Detective Zueger asked.

"No." Courtney was glad she and Alex went over the guests' movements, which made some of the questions easier to answer. "He worked in the back yard, cleaning up and getting the area ready for our guests to sit out there once it's a little warmer, or even on these warm days.

"Alex and I went out there to see how much progress had been made and if the supplies Braden needed were arriving on time. We were with him, and then he got some food from Willow. When Kris called and said Phil hadn't come to pick her up in Elm City, he left to give her a ride back here."

"Sounds like you believe he's innocent."

She didn't hesitate. "Yes. He's a pragmatic man and knows enough about the world to know the money is gone. And he didn't leave here during the time Phil was killed."

"Which doesn't mean he wouldn't seek revenge," Sheriff Warren said.

Courtney shook her head. "He worked too hard when he got out of prison to risk going back. He told me he went to Detective Zueger about Phil's scam, so you know more than I do. Did he seem revengeful to you?"

The sheriff stared at her. "I can't tell you what the detectives shared. It might hinder their investigation."

"From where I'm sitting, I don't see much investigation happened until all these people got together and came here. Is that what triggered him to act? Did he need a death to move forward with the inquiry?" She knew her voice rose at the end, and Nathan put his hand on her arm.

"I'm sorry it got to this point." Sheriff Warren's weary voice and drooping eyelids showed his feelings. "But it's too late to turn back the clock, and I'm sure the detective did everything he could to move forward as quickly as the law allows. It's unfair to blame him for the death."

Courtney took a deep breath in and let it out, trying to relax. He wasn't going to tell her what they'd done before this week. No point in asking again. As he said, they couldn't go back in time.

"What else did you want to confirm?" Nathan had been silent, probably because they hadn't asked anything about Courtney or Alex.

"What do you know about Melanie's movements yesterday?"

Courtney decided to start with lunchtime. If he wanted to know about the morning, he could ask. "She ate lunch with us. Then she went driving for about a half hour with Jade, and they came back because of Melanie's appointment with Dr. Alois. Afterwards, Melanie went to her room. I didn't see her again, but her vehicle was in the parking lot."

"So, she might have gone out with someone else?"

She considered everyone's movements. "Well, Kris was out already, so not with her. Melanie went out with her car at about the same time Jade and Lauren left. Melanie came back in time to see Clarissa at 2:30. After she went back to her room, I don't remember seeing her the rest of the afternoon until we ate in the evening. She's the quiet one of the bunch. I've hardly noticed she's here."

Sheriff Warren's face remained a mask as he rifled through the pages. "And to confirm…Rory and Ivy left right after lunch, and you didn't see them again until later that evening."

"Right."

"Any idea where the gun came from in Jade's room?"

The question came as a surprise. She glanced at Nathan.

He shrugged, which meant he didn't care if she answered.

"I only have speculations, but I have no knowledge. I didn't see anyone going into Jade's room." She hesitated. Running ideas past Alex didn't mean she wanted to say them to the police. It didn't feel right.

"You know something." He stated it as a fact.

She shook her head, her hair flaring out. "I don't. Alex and I were guessing about who could get into her room. Their keycards only open the front door and their own rooms."

"You're avoiding answering." He settled back like he'd wait all day.

Tired of his questions, she wanted him to leave now. Phil had only been killed yesterday, and it felt like months since it happened.

"You can guess as well as we did. The staff have access. As far as the guests…if two of them are working together, one could distract Jade, and the other could place the gun there. It doesn't exclude anyone."

He looked thoughtful. "Two of them working together would complicate things."

"It would," Nathan agreed.

"We've covered everything for right now."

She didn't appreciate him adding "right now."

"I'll grab my papers and leave you to your guests." He smiled at her. He was approachable when his expression relaxed. She liked him and knew he had to follow the rules.

"And you've cleared both Alex and Courtney of this murder, right?" Nathan asked.

"They're no longer suspects. But if two people conspired, I haven't ruled out Braden. A friendly warning." He shuffled their papers together and stood.

She took his words to mean she should be careful around Braden. "I'll keep it in mind, but I can't see why Braden would go to Detective Zueger in the first place if he decided to kill Phil."

"Maybe the situation changed." He walked to the door.

She followed with Nathan behind her.

"Thank you for your time." He nodded at her and Nathan.

The hallway was empty as they traversed it to the front door. She could hear Willow in the kitchen, but otherwise the place was quiet, with no one in the great room as they said goodbye. Courtney watched from the dining room window as the sheriff pulled out and drove away.

"They're gone. I suppose I should go back to Bismarck," Nathan said, throwing his arm around her shoulders.

She turned to look at him. "Don't you want a vacation?"

He laughed. "You want me to stay and keep away the big, bad wolf?"

"I've got Alex. I thought you might want a break."

"It's not possible, and this was a break for me. Things have piled up while I've been here. I'm taking time off for Paul's wedding and will be back. I need to catch up now, so I can enjoy their special weekend."

She sighed. "I miss you guys. I don't get to see anybody anymore."

"Who chose to live way out here?" he chided and flicked a finger under her chin.

"You're right." She brightened up. "I do love it out here."

He looked around before he spoke. "Even with a murderer on the loose?"

"Even with. They'll all be gone soon."

"Unless Braden is part of it. Don't discount him because you like him." His voice was as serious as Sheriff Warren's had been. "Call if either of you need me. I'll come as fast as I can get here."

"I know you will." She hugged him, and then he walked away to go pack.

She held back the tears. She would be too busy to miss him for long, and he would be back to visit in a few weeks for the wedding.

CHAPTER 34

Dr. Clarissa Alois had talked to a few murderers in her time as a psychologist. She sat in her office waiting for the first of the guests to come for his appointment: Rory Campbell. Clarissa saw, underneath Rory's displays of affection for his wife, he was a worried man.

Of course, having been informed all the guests either had a relative lose money or lost money themselves to Phil Young probably explained the worry. She'd wait and see what Rory said.

He entered the room and plopped down on the chair across from her. His bulky frame made it hard to slouch, but somehow he gave that impression. In fact, Clarissa wondered if he'd played on a football team in his high school years.

"So, I guess I have to be here," Rory said.

"Bosses' orders," Clarissa agreed. She was used to all sorts, and it took a lot to throw her. Besides, with her experience, she usually had some idea which patients to be wary of during her time with them. "Don't you have anything you'd like to talk over?"

"I have to tell you, Doc, I don't plan to say much. I told Ivy not to say anything either." He sounded like an aggrieved child.

"I see. Do you have a reason for not wanting to talk? Don't you want to take this opportunity to unload your frustration?" She kept her tone even and noncommittal.

"You could use it against us in court, and neither Ivy nor I have any money left since…" he paused. "Well, since *he* ripped us off. Now Ivy has to go back to work full-time."

"Everything you say is confidential. I can't tell the police what you say."

"There's always a way."

"I see." He wouldn't listen to her reassurances the appointment was confidential, so she went back to his grievance. "And that wasn't your plan for Ivy to go back to work?"

"No." Rory relaxed and leaned forward. "We were going to put a downpayment on a house, and she would stay home with our children, as soon as we had some."

"She wanted to quit work then?"

"Yes. That's what we wanted." He let out a big sigh. "With Phil dead, there's no way we're going to get our money back. The police are involved, and I bet they've frozen all his assets, and none of us are going to get a penny. I wish I knew who sent Phil the anonymous text to get him here."

"You didn't have to come to the inn, even though the others were coming. You and Ivy could have stayed home and not been involved."

Rory jerked back and let out a snort. "I have to say, Doc, you're kind of naive. The only way we would get our share was to follow the others. They were looking out for themselves."

"Then why would someone kill him? As you said, there won't be enough money to go around."

"Well…see, this is where I should stop talking. You'll share what I say with the police." Rory sank back again and closed his lips tightly.

Clarissa shook her head and tried again to explain confidentiality. "I can't share anything you say to me. Even though you're not paying for this session, it is considered a psychiatric consultation under patient confidentiality laws. If you confess to a murder, I can't report you. The only thing I could tell the police is if you're planning to hurt someone or yourself in the future."

Rory sat there silently. He finally shook his head. "I'm done. I'll sit here until the time is up."

"Your choice."

Rory sat silently, arms across his chest.

A timid knock sounded on the door, and Rory got up and opened it. When he saw Ivy, he said, "Don't say anything."

She watched him walk away and then looked at Clarissa with wary eyes, scanning her face.

CHAPTER 35

"Come in," Clarissa said.

Ivy closed the door, walked slowly over to the chair in front of her desk and sat down. Unlike her husband, she didn't slouch. She sat up like she was ready for the starting gun in a race, like she wanted to leap into action and run out of the room.

"Rory told me not to talk to you," she said, hands clenched in her lap.

"Do you want to talk to me?" She relaxed against the back of her chair and looked at Ivy calmly.

"I do. There's no one else I can talk to except Rory. He tells me to take it easy. Everything will work out fine." She reached up and grabbed the arms of the chair, digging her fingernails into the leather. "Well, it's not fine. It won't be fine, but he doesn't get it."

"What do you think is going to happen that won't work out?"

"We're suspects. What if they never find the murderer? We'll be suspects the rest of our lives. How am I supposed to find a job? Rory doesn't understand." Now she seemed ready to levitate out of the chair.

"We were going to buy a house, and then Rory decided we needed to invest the money we had. He said it was a sure thing, and he'd gotten a tip to invest with Phil." Bitterness dripped from her tongue. "A sure thing. I love Rory, but sometimes he is gullible. Before I knew it, he gave Phil the money. I'd told Rory to wait and check out the guy, but, no, he always knows better." She paused to take a breath.

Clarissa waited to see if she was done or wanted to continue. The answer came quickly.

"We were going to have a house," she wailed. "An actual house. With neighbors outside our walls. Our walls. Not apartment walls. A parking spot and garage and a yard where our children can play. Rory doesn't know it yet, but I'm pregnant." She put her hands over her tummy and shrank into the chair. It seemed to suck her into its depths.

"I'm pregnant. When am I going to tell him? On the way back from our trip? If we're suspects, the police aren't going to leave us alone because I'm having a baby. This was supposed to be a happy time. Rory said we should go to the shooting range to soften up Phil. What a waste of time. Kris already promised to get us our money back. As soon as she gave us the money, I planned to tell Rory about the baby.

"The police aren't going to release any money, and that's the end. No money and going back to work full-time with a baby. Life's great." She sat with a pout on her lips.

Time passed, and Clarissa gave Ivy the chance to process what she'd shared. She'd finally run out of words.

"I'm sorry things didn't work out for you and Rory with the financial situation. It must be hard to keep the baby a secret from him. Do you feel better? Would it help to talk with him when I'm in the room?"

Ivy looked at Clarissa like she'd forgotten she was sitting there. Then she smiled. "Thank you. I do feel better for spewing all that out. I guess I did need to tell someone. I appreciate your offer, but I need to tell him when we're alone. He would already be upset I told you this much."

"Are you afraid of him?"

Ivy laughed sweetly. "He's a softie. He puts on the big guy show. No, he wouldn't hurt me."

"Okay. Remember, my door is open if I don't have another appointment, and the sessions are free."

Her lips twisted. "Yeah. One free thing. But you were helpful. Thank you." She got up and went to the door. "I'll be back."

Clarissa smiled at Ivy. "Anytime."

She left and passed Lauren coming in the door.

"Have a chair," she said.

She plopped down in the chair Ivy vacated. Lauren looked at home. No twisting hands or tapping feet. No irritation.

"We talked yesterday about your previous visits with a psychologist. How are you doing today after everything?"

"Oh, it's been interesting and scary at the same time. I'm not happy about being a suspect in a murder." She shrugged. "I have nothing to hide and haven't killed anyone."

"So, you didn't kill Phil?" Clarissa tried to shake her calm.

She laughed. "No. I'm not that lost." Lauren leaned forward. "I'm trying to find out who did though."

CHAPTER 36

"You're investigating Mr. Young's death?" Clarissa asked Lauren. Alarm coursed through her chest. Didn't Lauren know how dangerous her actions could be?

"I want to know who did it. I don't want this hanging over my head for the rest of my life. Besides, I could write a true crime book out of it. I haven't tried nonfiction yet. It might be interesting." She pursed her lips together, and her gaze lost focus.

Clarissa waited her out. Lauren could use the time however she wanted to spend it.

"I hope it's not Aunt Kris. How awkward. The family wouldn't want me to write about it."

Her comment said a lot about her, if she only realized it. She seemed lost in her make-believe world of writing a book about the murder.

She got a vibe from Lauren she hadn't gotten from Rory or Ivy. Not a guilty vibe exactly, but something different. She wasn't sure if her years of experience as a psychologist suggested the idea.

"Are you feeling depressed out here in the middle of nowhere?" she asked.

She threw Clarissa an incredulous look. "You live here."

"Out of choice, yes."

"Well, I had a choice, but not much of one. I came to make sure the rest of the group didn't revile Aunt Kris along with Uncle Phil. Since none of us knew who sent the anonymous text to Phil, I thought I should come and keep an eye on everybody for her. I guess I didn't do such a great job. Although how could I know someone schemed to kill him?

"And Jade appeared more sad than angry. At least I thought so. When we discovered she had a gun, we were stunned. The police must not know whose gun someone used to kill Uncle Phil because they haven't arrested anyone yet.

"We have only a few more days here, and then everyone leaves. I hope the police find the person responsible." Lauren finished with a defeated shrug.

"Maybe the police know more than they're saying," Clarissa suggested. "It's only been two days. I'm sure they must have to check out a lot of things."

She shrugged. "I hope they know more than I do."

"Aren't you concerned about who it might be? I thought you liked your Aunt Kris, Jade, and Melanie. What if it's one of them?"

She smiled. "Not if they're a killer. And Aunt Kris? I doubt it. She doesn't benefit in any way from Uncle Phil's death. His bad deeds are coming out. There will be a lot of talk in Minot. It may be a city, but it's a small city. Besides, if the police freeze all their assets, she won't have much to live on, which wouldn't suit her. No, she's smart and crafty and would never do something that would bring more bad stuff down on her. She would have quietly taken over the reins from Uncle Phil without him knowing it.”

“You make her sound like a scheming woman.”

“Well, let’s just say, I don’t believe she’s exactly as innocent or unknowledgeable as she claims. I kept her up-to-date, and she knew the police were closing in. It was a matter of time. But I love her.”

“You make her sound awful, and yet you love her.”

“She was available when I was depressed, and no one else stuck around. She got me through some rough times, so, yes, I love her.” Lauren stared at her in defiance.

“An excellent reason.” She thought Lauren deflated a little when she realized Clarissa wasn’t going to argue with her. “What about Jade and Skylar?”

“If I said their uncle killing himself is a good enough reason to murder Uncle Phil for his part, I would be lying. I’ve been depressed in the past. For all I know, their uncle was depressed, and Uncle Phil’s actions were the last straw. I don’t know about blaming someone else enough to kill yourself. I’d be more likely to kill the person harming me than killing myself in that situation.”

“We never know, do we?” Clarissa asked.

“No. No one knows what someone else is feeling.” Her lips drooped, and her eyes dropped to her hands.

"Do you want to talk about it?" Was Lauren as okay as she claimed?

Lauren looked up at her, her face composed once more. "About what?"

"Depression? Your aunt? Your uncle?"

"No. I don't think it would help." She got up from the chair. "It's time for some other lucky person to sit here. Thank you for letting me say those things and not treating me patronizingly because I said I'd been depressed."

"It's not a moral failing," she assured her.

"No. It's not." She turned and left the room, closing the door behind her.

Clarissa pondered her words about killing the person causing the problems instead of killing themselves. Depending on one's personality, the choice could go either way. Of course, Hank was dead, but Jade and Skylar, who cared about him, were here.

Another knock sounded, and the door opened.

CHAPTER 37

"Hello. I'm supposed to come see you for a half hour," Kris said to Clarissa as she entered her office and closed the door. Her gray hair hung limply, and her pale blue eyes listlessly roamed around the room. "There's not much you can do for me."

"Well, I can't change the last three days, if that's what you're asking. Maybe it would help you to speak about whatever you want. I'm an objective outsider."

She stood by the door.

"Why don't you start by taking a chair? You don't have to talk. You can sit there." Clarissa motioned to the chair in front of her desk, sympathizing with the woman who lost her husband and was dealing with the fallout of Phil's scams by herself.

Kris approached the chair like it might bite her and sat down. "All I've been doing lately is sitting and thinking."

"Have you talked it over with anyone?" she asked. "Your niece?"

"With Lauren? With those other jackals who were out for Phil's hide and got him?" Her eyes filled with tears. "You know, I loved him. Well, I love him. He's not here to love anymore."

She pulled a tissue from the box beside the chair and wiped her eyes. Her gaze wandered around the room, and then she pulled herself up and sat straight in the chair. "You can't tell anyone what I say, right?"

"Right."

"Including police, and Alex and Courtney, right?" she insisted.

"Right. I can't, and I won't," she assured Kris and waited for her confession. Whatever was on her mind bothered her enough to confess it.

It took five minutes of her biting her lips, then pursing them, and then biting them again. Clarissa waited patiently.

"When he received the anonymous text telling him to book a room, I convinced him to come. I knew the police were close to serving a search warrant." Her gaze became sharp and focused, and she stared at Clarissa. "I didn't want to be there to see the police go through everything. I didn't want Phil to be there either. He was soft in the center and had no backbone. It would have killed him to realize his dreams were over. He wasn't going to get away with it, whatever he'd been doing.

"It's my fault he's dead. If I hadn't convinced him to come, he wouldn't have been here and wouldn't have been killed. I never expected any of these kids would have the courage to shoot him."

"Yet one of those 'kids' threatened him that morning," Clarissa reminded her.

She sniffed with contempt. "Jade. She had no guts. Phil told me she couldn't pull the trigger."

Clarissa wanted to say the threat should have warned her people weren't always what they looked like on the outside.

Kris shrugged. "Like it mattered. Someone else shot him anyway."

"Unless it was Jade, and then she left."

Kris shook her head. "Once you wimp out, you don't try again. At least not right away. She would have to rebuild her courage."

She sounded like she spoke from personal knowledge. Clarissa hoped she hadn't killed anyone. As she wasn't threatening anyone right now, there was nothing she could say to anyone about this conversation due to patient confidentiality laws.

Kris's tears dried on her face. Her eyes were red-rimmed and slightly outlined in black from smeared makeup.

"Did the police search upset you?"

She gave Clarissa a scornful look. "Of course. I didn't like someone touching all my stuff. They took Phil's papers away with them. At least they left my stuff here. I don't want to sleep in that room again."

"Why don't you let Courtney know? Maybe she can move you to Jade's room, since she's gone. Would that bother you?"

"No. It would be fine. What a good idea."

"I'm sure Courtney and Skylar would help you move, although I don't know if you want anyone else touching your possessions."

"I don't have much. I can do it myself." She was perking up from their talk, and Clarissa saw a spark return to her eyes. It wouldn't last long, but for now, she would be fine.

"You know you didn't kill Phil by bringing him here, don't you?" she asked.

She twisted the tissue into shreds. "It feels like I did."

"It's quite possible the same thing might have happened in Minot at some later time."

"Maybe."

She stopped talking then—it seemed she'd said all she wanted to say. She'd confessed to her part in their travel plans, and now she would be thinking of what the police would do next. As with Lauren, Clarissa had the feeling there was plenty more she could say about the situation. Aunt and niece were a lot alike.

CHAPTER 38

Clarissa looked at her watch after Kris left. She had a half hour free because of Jade's absence. She was surprised by another knock on the door. Whoever it was didn't come in, so she got up to see what they needed. Probably Alex or Courtney, but they would have texted.

She opened it to find Hugh with a tray filled with sandwiches, fruit, water, and a cookie. There were two of each, so he planned to join her. "Wow. What a nice treat. Come in."

"Courtney told me your break time. I thought you'd need some fuel." He set the tray on a side conference table, and they sat down.

"Thank you. These cookies better be fresh-baked after the day I've had."

Her husband chuckled. "Not to make light of your clients' issues, but I take it there were issues." He took one of the plates with a sandwich, a bowl of fruit, and a fork. "So, how is it going?" he asked as Clarissa took her own share of the food and a glass of water from the tray.

"Pretty good. It's been interesting. There are times I wish I could tell the police a few helpful things. Unfortunately for the police, I can't. Fortunately for the patient, it's good. They get things off their minds. They need to relieve the internal pressure."

"I know what you mean. Even when I'm spiritually guiding people, I feel like it helps their physical problems. If I know there's more going on, I refer them, but they are afraid to seek help, and I can't report what I don't know."

"At least you have more leeway in reporting. I don't." Having eaten her fruit and half her sandwich already, she realized how hungry she'd been.

"Oh, the fun of being a psychologist. As a deacon, I have a code to follow." Hugh munched on his cookie. "It's a good thing we moved out here. There's such a need for clergy and spiritual help in these rural areas. And it's beautiful here."

"I know I've hardly seen you since we got back from Bismarck. Can you believe we're in the midst of a murder investigation?" she asked after she finished her sandwich.

"No. This was supposed to be a peaceful atmosphere. Work during the day. Come home in the evening and relax on the deck in the prairie moonlight. Or sunlight." He smiled at her. "The murder could affect Alex and Courtney's business. I'm not concerned about our investment. I believe God will work it out for us. At least these guests will be gone in a few days and relieve the pressure on the rest of us while we get ready for Paul's wedding. I hope they solve the murder before long, so it doesn't cause any more problems for the innocent."

She nodded thoughtfully. "Yes. This situation we've agreed to with Alex and Courtney has sure started out with—"

"Don't say it. It's not funny." Hugh smiled. "A bang."

He laughed. "You're such a child. If only your patients could see this side of you instead of the neutral expression you use to treat them."

"I do not use a neutral expression to treat them. I use a listening expression. They'd never talk to me if I didn't seem approachable." She grabbed the cookie he'd left on the tray for her and took a small bite. "These do taste good."

"I'll tell Willow you liked them. She baked them, so you can find more in the kitchen. You have a busy schedule today."

A knock sounded on the door. "My next patient, and since you'll know by seeing her anyway, I can say it's Willow. Now, take your tray and get out of my office." She smiled at him. "Thank you."

He stood up and leaned over to hug her as she gathered the remnants of their meal. "I love you."

She stopped and kissed him. "I love you too."

She went to the door to open it for Hugh, who carried the tray. Hugh and Willow smiled at each other, and then Clarissa closed the door behind him.

CHAPTER 39

Willow continued to smile as she took a chair across from Clarissa where she sat behind her desk. "Well, here we are."

"Here we are." Clarissa smiled back. "Thanks for the lunch. It was perfect, with an excellent cookie to finish the meal."

"Thank you." Willow seemed pleased at the praise. She'd been busy in the kitchen ever since the guests arrived. Clarissa thought she must be tired.

As far as Clarissa learned from the reports she'd gotten from Alex and Courtney, Willow was the least likely to have killed Phil. As far as anyone knew, she'd been one of the few who didn't know the guests met in Minot until Phil's death brought out the information. Clarissa didn't sense anything about Willow to dispute the theory. So far, she was the most relaxed and natural-appearing person Clarissa had seen today.

"So, I have an alibi for the whole time needed, and I don't feel like I need to be here." Willow settled back against the chair, relaxed.

"I've heard. Are you concerned at all about the people around you? Scared or suspicious of anyone? This meeting is to make sure you're comfortable working here. If not, I'm sure Alex and Courtney can manage until everyone leaves."

She shook her head, smiling. "Honestly? I don't think they can get by without me right now. I've spent a lot of time in the kitchen. If it weren't for the fact I'm going to be behind because of this half hour, I'd be happy sitting here."

"Do you resent being busy?"

She shrugged and remained relaxed. "It's my life. I've always been busy, and I like it that way."

What or who was she running from? No one who kept moving as Willow did liked it. "What do you do for fun when you have the energy?"

"I've forgotten." She laughed. "Look. I know you, Alex and Courtney are concerned, but truly, I'm okay. I'm not scared of anyone. I don't know anything that could harm anyone. I have no idea who killed Phil."

"Your window looks out on the parking lot. You might have seen someone coming or going at the wrong time."

"Hardly. I rarely have time to look out the window."

"But maybe you do often enough? Wouldn't you notice if a vehicle was gone for a while?" She hated to press the issue, but Willow's lack of self-preservation in this situation concerned her. She didn't want her to fear everyone, but healthy caution would be good.

Willow sat there quietly. "You know, the police never asked me. It's kind of odd. You're right though. I do occasionally look out the window. It's beautiful outside. I like the space of the prairie and the crocuses all over the grassy area where I can see them outside the window. I imagine they'll be gone soon. Then there will be yellow dandelions, which I like, despite most people considering them weeds. Who hasn't given their mother a handful of dandelions when they were young?"

"Do you have family in town?" she asked.

"Not anymore. My aunt lived here for years, but she died a few years ago. When I graduated from college, I wanted to live in a rural area. I didn't believe I'd find a place to work, and then I saw the advertisement for this job. The internet pictures of the area convinced me to come back."

"So, you'll stay around?" She arranged her chair closer to the desk and leaned her elbows on the surface.

"At least for a few years."

"And you're sure you're not afraid?"

"I wasn't, but you're starting to convince me I should be," she said ruefully.

"I want you to be cautious. That's all." She'd made a mess of this visit for sure. "I wanted to double-check you were okay. And you are. Two days and everyone will be gone."

"You're right. I'm fine." She relaxed again. "Can we sit quietly the rest of the time? I'm tired."

"Sure. I'll read this book I have here." She pulled a book over from behind her laptop. Willow did look wiped out. Clarissa would have to talk to Courtney about help for Willow in the kitchen. She couldn't continue this pace every week.

"Great." Willow leaned her head against the back of the chair and closed her eyes.

CHAPTER 40

Skylar rushed into Clarissa's office and plopped down on the chair in front of her desk. She gave her an impish grin and said, "Hi."

"Hello. You don't seem too upset about what's going on. In fact, I'd say you're enjoying it." She sensed the change before Skylar's face registered wide eyes.

"You're wrong. I'm terrified. Terrified the killer is someone I know. The only person I feel safe with is Willow." Her voice shook at the end. "I heard she has an alibi, and she's busy in the kitchen. Someone would have noticed if she left."

Which probably explained her smile when she came in. She'd passed Willow in the hall. She shouldn't have jumped in with her thoughts and let Skylar take the lead. But, on second thought, it brought them right where she wanted them to be.

"How do you deal with being afraid?" Clarissa asked.

"I avoid being alone with anyone if I can. I stay out of everyone's way and do my job. I wish Courtney hadn't needed me so much this week. I would have been happy staying home with my kids and Mom until the guests were all gone."

Clarissa kept her mouth shut, waiting for her to continue.

She bit her fingernail and looked at it. "I don't know what else to say."

"Whatever you want to talk about is fine."

"I don't have anything to talk about."

She sensed Skylar did have something to say. "Do you have an idea about who killed Phil? Is that why you're scared?"

"We all thought it was Braden. He's the one who had the job here first, and he and Lauren got us all together."

"How did it happen you all got together? How did Braden and Lauren know who to contact?"

"I think Lauren snuck into her uncle's office and found some information. I didn't ask her directly, but she probably took information and started looking for relatives of the older people who were Phil's victims. I don't trust her anymore. I didn't know Phil was her uncle." A puzzled look crossed her face.

She sensed Skylar could tell her more if she chose. "What does your mom think of you working here at the moment with what's going on?"

She wore the expression again where her eyes squinted together, and she frowned. "She's not concerned at all, which surprises me. She's been very much in my business ever since I returned to live with her. Before these guests arrived, she asked question after question about who came and what I did during the day.

"Of course, she was interested because this is a new business, so I put it down to that. All of Elm City is curious about anything new, and they wanted details. I'm sure my mom had lots of her friends quizzing her about the place after I'd been here the first time." She paused for a minute.

Clarissa let silence fill the room.

"You know, it's interesting talking about this because I realized, since Phil's murder, she doesn't ask me much. Which is weird. I would want to know even more if I were her." She lapsed into silence again, considering her mother's weirdness, Clarissa assumed.

She also thought it was strange because, if it were her daughter working here, she'd be asking more questions after the murder. She'd want to know her child was safe.

"Well, I don't know," Skylar finally said and shrugged. "Whatever. I guess the novelty wore off. Or maybe it's because we spent Monday together, so I didn't know what happened until later. She could be talking to people in town about the murder."

"Which is probably true. After all, it happened out in the country and not at the inn. Did you see Kris in town during the day while she waited for Phil to pick her up?" Clarissa asked.

"I didn't. But Mom said she saw her in the grocery store that day. It must have been while Kris wandered around Elm City waiting for Phil to come back and pick her up. Mom took a different aisle to avoid Kris. Kris came out to see Mom a few months ago about Uncle Hank and offered Mom money. My mom screamed at her and told her money doesn't bring back a dead man.

"Mom took forever to pick up the chocolate chips she went to buy for the cookies we were making. She said she ran into some friends and talked for a while. I know she watches my kids a lot, and the errand allowed her to get away and talk to someone besides me or the kids. I didn't begrudge her the time. I'm happy she's willing to watch the kids for me while I'm working. Plus, she kept trying to avoid Kris."

"That is nice to have her in the same town. Is that why you decided to move here?"

Her mouth firmed. "Part of the reason. Since Mom lives in town and is willing to watch the kids, I save on daycare. It's hard making enough to pay for daycare and have money to buy groceries and other necessities. When Mom told me she'd heard through the grapevine Courtney and Alex were hiring, I applied right away.

"I'm not sure what's going to happen if I can't work here." She brightened up. "Well, I'm not going to worry right now. I know Alex's brother is getting married here in a few weeks, so at least I'll have a job until then."

Clarissa thought Skylar was a glass-half-full person. Then someone knocked on the door. She looked at the old-fashioned crystal watch on her wrist.

CHAPTER 41

Skylar bounced up from the chair in Clarissa's office, the same way she sat down when she came into the room. "Your next appointment. Thank you."

"You're welcome."

Skylar hurried to the door. Did she always do everything at top speed? Maybe all her energy came from caring for two young children. Although, she thought most mothers of two small children spent more time tired than energetic.

"Before you go," she stopped her mid-stride, "is there anything else concerning you?"

She turned around and stared at Clarissa vacantly. "Why? What could be concerning me?"

"Well, are you afraid?"

A slight hesitation followed, and then she said, "No. I'm fine." She turned around and left.

Clarissa felt a moment of disquiet, but she put it aside. She heard Braden greet Skylar in the hallway, and then Braden was in the room, closing the door behind him.

He didn't bounce or stride. He slowly made his way to the chair where everyone else sat and lowered himself heavily. Wariness showed in his eyes.

"Hi, Braden." Clarissa straightened a few things on her desk that didn't need repositioned, trying to relax her reluctant visitor.

"Hi. This is kind of weird." Avoiding eye contact, Braden looked around the room. "I haven't seen this room since we finished construction."

So, he wouldn't talk about the murder unless Clarissa asked.

"No. Security has to be tight, but I know we're making small talk here. You know why it's locked all the time," she said.

Braden's gaze turned toward her. "Yes. I know why. Confidentiality. It makes me feel better about talking to you today, but I'm afraid anything I say might get back to the police."

"If you want reassurance, I can tell you, legally and morally, there are only a few reasons I can share any information from this appointment. I stick to my morals."

Braden was another one with something on his mind. Guilt, maybe? But for a murder? Or for telling everyone he worked here, and someone taking advantage of that fact?

The murderer was clever to use the situation to their advantage by bringing all the suspects to one place. She didn't envy the police their search for the guilty party. Although, if honest with herself, she found the challenge of talking to the suspects and guessing which one had the potential to plan this murder challenging. She pushed away the shameful thought.

"It certainly sounded like you meant I'd planned Phil's death." He leaned forward, finally engaged in the conversation. "I did not murder him. I was not in on any plot, and I don't know who did it." He pulled at his hair and then dropped his hand.

"I'm angry, if you want to know my true emotion right now. Angry at whoever is messing up my life."

"Messing up your life? I thought they cleared you?" Clarissa asked.

"Oh, they cleared me with an alibi. They believe I might have been in on some plan. And, second, I just got out of prison. Alex gave me this job. He trusted me. I don't know if he still does. He and I need to talk, but the police have been swarming the place, and Alex has been busy. I told him yesterday, but his attorney was there too. I don't know what he thinks now. I told people I worked here. I didn't tell someone to send an anonymous text and bring everybody running to harass Phil into returning the money he stole." He pulled at his hair again.

"My mom has said goodbye to her money and made peace with the idea. I'm not quite as happy about the situation, but she's right. It's not possible to ever get her investment back. Which burns me up. And all those other people who lost money too. And I don't buy for a minute Kris didn't know anything."

"What do you mean?" Clarissa asked, intrigued by Braden's angry words.

"Lauren talked to her after she and I first discussed the situation. She's known for at least two months. And so have the police. If the police did something sooner, none of this would have happened, and my job wouldn't be in jeopardy. Just because my mother has accepted the loss of money doesn't mean I can lose my income. Anything could happen, and ex-cons don't find jobs easily." He'd finally wound down and leaned back again in his chair, although his hand occasionally reached for his hair before he dropped it back onto his leg.

"There's a lot to process," Clarissa said. Poor guy. If innocent, he didn't deserve to be put in this position. A lot of people didn't.

"I finally found a job with a place to stay and thought I was set." His shoulders slumped.

"Don't give up yet. Once Alex has time to process everything, he may keep you on here, and you won't lose your job." Clarissa thought, if Braden wasn't guilty, Alex would keep him on as groundskeeper at the inn. He would be aware of the consequences if he let Braden, an ex-convict, go, and he wasn't a vindictive man. Alex was generous and understanding. Alex's own time in prison, taking the blame for something he didn't do, made him aware of Braden's precarious position.

"I hope so." He sounded defeated.

"Try to keep from thinking about the what-ifs and take it one day at a time."

"You're right." He squared his shoulders. "I need to talk to Alex again, and maybe if I can find out who killed Phil, that will help."

Clarissa's heart jumped into her throat, which wasn't physically possible, but it felt like her heart lodged there. Here was another person who wanted to investigate. Were all the innocent people trying to solve Phil's murder?

"You shouldn't be searching for a dangerous murderer. Let the police do their job dealing with the situation." She knew how ironic her words were because she'd been trying to figure out the guilty party herself.

"Do you feel like you want to talk longer today? I can take the time. Or you could come back if that's more convenient."

"No. I'm fine."

Clarissa's face expressed her doubt.

"Really." Braden smiled for the first time since he entered the room. "I promise to come see you if I'm depressed or upset and need someone to talk to."

"You do that. I'm here for you."

"Is our time up today?" Braden asked.

Clarissa looked again at the watch Hugh had given her. "A few minutes left, but we're close enough to the half hour, if you want to leave, you can."

Braden didn't exactly jump up from the chair, but he moved faster than when he'd come into the room. Halfway to the door, Clarissa stopped him.

"Braden. Be careful."

Her grave tone must have gotten through to Braden because he frowned, then said, "I will. Promise."

Clarissa sat there after Braden left. She worried the young man didn't realize what could happen if he continued to look for the killer. A killer who used a whole group of people to accomplish their goal.

She suddenly felt wary and scared for a few of the people she'd talked to. The guests were going

to investigate and put themselves in harm's way.
And so were Courtney and Alex.

CHAPTER 42

The last person scheduled to meet with Clarissa was Melanie. Her knock, if it was Melanie, was quick and soft. If she hadn't been waiting for her, she might not have noticed.

She let Melanie into the room, and she went straight to the chair in front of Clarissa's desk. When she'd talked with her yesterday, they hadn't found Phil yet and didn't even know he was dead.

When they both settled, Clarissa asked, "Since I know you all came to the inn because of Phil, I have to ask about yesterday's session. Did you make up what you told me?"

Melanie's head jerked up, her face flushed as she met Clarissa's gaze. "No. I went through everything I told you. I might be one of the only people here this week who wanted to get help. I had another reason for coming related to Phil."

Clarissa waited for her to continue, relieved she hadn't misread Melanie yesterday and believed a bunch of lies. She'd been honest about her trials with her first husband's death and her guilt over her budding relationship with another man.

She wrapped her arms around herself as if she were cold. "I have some law enforcement relatives. I didn't tell any of them what was going on with Phil before this week, which I now regret." Her laugh was forced.

"I don't know if it would have made any difference if I had told them," she continued. "They might have told the Minot police, but if someone planned to kill Phil, it would have been hard to stop them. Plus, I didn't realize someone's agenda. The whole bunch of them were acting like vigilantes, and I thought I could at least be here and stop them from getting carried away. Like I said, in the end, it didn't matter. No one except Jade and the killer had time to do anything. My presence didn't stop anything," she muttered.

"You don't know that," Clarissa said. "I saw you talking to Jade and Lauren. Maybe you kept them occupied enough not to carry things further, if they're innocent."

She hung her head and then lifted it again to stare directly at her. "I have a confession to make. I put the gun in Jade's room."

Clarissa managed to keep her face impassive, despite the surprise revelation. Melanie would have been her last guess. "Why?"

"I never told you yesterday, but my husband was murdered in a drive-by shooting. Ever since then, I've carried a weapon. It was kind of a security blanket." She dropped her eyes. "I know it sounds stupid."

"It's not stupid. It's normal to want to feel safe. Did they solve your husband's death?"

"No. It's unsolved." Tears appeared in her eyes. "I'll probably never know what happened to him. About the gun…I told Jade I wanted to hide it in her room after Phil was killed, because I was afraid of being a suspect. She agreed. She was leaving anyway. They couldn't trace the gun to her or me, as I never registered it. I won't say where I got the gun, but it's going to come out now. I'll probably be in some kind of trouble over admitting it's mine. Anyway, Jade and I snuck it into her room before she left."

She unwrapped her arms from around her waist and rested them on the chair. "I planned to get it back before Courtney or Alex found it. I'm sorry they got caught up in it."

Clarissa thought back to Jade's hurried goodbye. "Wasn't she afraid you were the killer?"

Melanie shook her head. "It hadn't been used, and Jade knew by sniffing at it. Her uncle taught her a lot about guns. Plus, I overheard Alex tell Courtney the murder weapon was found on the ground by Phil. Jade promised to keep everything to herself and trusted me. From the little I know about her, she hasn't had an easy life, and Hank's death shook her."

"How do you know?" Clarissa asked, processing this new information.

"We got together before we came to the inn—I assumed you knew. In the last two weeks, we were somewhat of a posse, meeting for the big event. Looking back, if Phil hadn't died, I would find our attempts for restitution somewhat funny. Not totally funny though."

"Did you know before this week Skylar and Jade were cousins?"

"I forgot. They didn't seem to get along when they were together. I'm not sure why. Maybe because they don't appear to have anything in common except Hank. Jade has the whole bad girl vibe going on, and Skylar has two children to raise. They both adore Skylar's mother, though. My memory is returning about a few things Jade said. About how she always felt at home with Skylar's mother. Maybe that was a source of tension. Jade wanted to have a mom like Skylar's and was jealous she didn't."

"How are you doing with everything going on with Phil's murder?"

Melanie wrapped her arms around herself again. "I'm tired of death. I want to leave, but somehow I feel I have to see this through. I couldn't be there for my husband, but maybe I can help someone here. Besides, I came to get away from my own life for a week, in addition to keeping everybody in line here.

"I don't know who killed Phil. I don't think it was Jade. She was too scared. As far as the others, Willow and Braden have alibis, and I can't see either one of them trusting someone else enough to be part of a team.

"Which leaves Rory and Ivy, and Kris and Lauren. Or a stranger who made use of the opportunity. Someone sent Phil the anonymous text. It must have been the murderer."

Melanie could be the guilty person, but Clarissa had been with her during the time of Phil's murder as far as she could tell from the timeline she'd heard. "I have a suggestion for you, since you've decided to stop your co-conspirators. How about confessing you gave Jade the gun, and you gave it to her to leave under the bed before she left?

It would at least answer one question for the police.”

Melanie silently studied her. “I suppose it’s an option. I wish Courtney’s brother, Nathan, was here. It would be nice to run it past a lawyer.”

“No lawyers in your family tree?” she asked.

She shook her head with a smile. “Law enforcement only.”

“How about telling one of them, and they can pass the information on to Sheriff Warren?”

Melanie thought for a minute. “Could work. I mean, I didn’t do anything wrong except hide a weapon without bullets in it. And it wasn’t the murder weapon.”

“Are your prints going to be on it?” she asked.

“No. I didn’t handle it with anything but a towel.”

“That’s taken care of. Do you want to talk about your situation and continue our discussion from yesterday?” She didn’t want to leave Melanie hanging on her personal issues.

“No. I’ve done enough talking today. Can we maybe get together tomorrow and talk about it instead of Phil?” she asked. “This is a chance I rarely get, and I want to deal with these problems for my daughter’s sake. Phil’s situation side-tracked me, but I can’t do anything else about his murder right now.”

“You want to though, don’t you?”

She laughed as she stood up. “Yes. I need to have things neat and orderly and taken care of.

Perhaps tomorrow we can talk about the reasons I need to control situations."

They made an appointment, and she promised to tell her law enforcement relative about the gun.

When she left, Clarissa sat there for a long time. She didn't realize how much time passed until there was another knock on the door. She didn't have any other appointments and had seen all the guests. Hugh hadn't texted her to ask if she was free. She had no idea who would want to see her again.

CHAPTER 43

Melanie stood on the other side of the door. "Can I come in for a minute?"

"Sure." Clarissa opened the door. Why had Melanie returned?

She stepped in and closed the door behind her but didn't make a move to sit down. "I should tell Alex and Courtney what I told you, but I don't want the whole place to know. How can we go about a secret meeting with them?"

"I can text them to see where they are, and we might be able to slip upstairs to their apartment and talk without anyone seeing us. Who is out there in the great room right now?" Clarissa asked.

"Lauren and Kris. Everyone else seems to have left to sightsee."

"Can they see the hallway from where they are?" she asked.

"No."

"Give me a second to text Alex and Courtney to find out if they have time now."

"Melanie in my office. Wants to share information with you but doesn't want to be seen. Are you available?" She sent the text.

A ding sounded almost immediately. She looked.

Alex replied, *"We're in our apartment. Let's meet in the stairwell, and we'll talk to her in our apartment."*

"They can see you now. Come with me." She slipped out of her office with Melanie following and led her down the hallway and around the corner to the staircase door. She entered the code and started up the stairway.

Alex met them about halfway. "Thanks, Clarissa." He smiled at her and Melanie.

Clarissa nodded. "I'll tell everyone else Melanie's having her meal in her room tonight, if anyone asks." She looked at Melanie. "Don't be afraid to tell them everything."

CHAPTER 44

Courtney stood by the door, waiting for Alex and Melanie, excited. Maybe it was something that would solve Phil's murder. When they reached the door, she said, "Hi, Melanie. Come in and have a chair."

Melanie looked around the apartment and chose a corner of the couch to sit on.

"Anybody want something to drink? Soda, water, tea?" Courtney asked.

"I'll get it," Alex said. "You all have a seat."

"I'll take a water," Courtney said.

"Me too," Melanie finally spoke.

Courtney could hardly wait for what Melanie would say. She plopped on the other side of the sofa from her.

Alex handed the water glasses to the women, put two coasters on the coffee table, and sat down. "Okay, we want to hear your story."

Melanie sat up straighter and stared at them through wide brown eyes. "I should have told you before, but it's been busy around here. The police were here, and you two were busy, and I didn't want anyone else to know."

She shared her information about Jade and the gun found under her bed. "I hoped to retrieve it before anyone saw it. I'm sorry it caused you problems with the sheriff. I'll be letting him know the gun is mine."

"Why did you bring the gun?" Alex asked.

"I always carry a gun with me. My husband was shot in a drive-by shooting, and I'm cautious now. I never dreamt someone would shoot Phil. It never crossed my mind.

"I wanted to stop the other guests from doing anything too wild. I certainly never anticipated someone would kill Phil the first day. After that, what could I do?" She looked at them beseechingly.

Moved by Melanie's disclosure about her husband, Courtney felt more sympathetic over the woman's confession about the gun. She patted Melanie on the back. "You did okay. It was a hard decision to make."

"I told Dr. Alois I'll be telling the police, a relative of mine, about the gun. I'm too chicken to confess directly to Sheriff Warren. My relative can pass the information on. By the time the sheriff gets back to questioning me, he'll have calmed down."

Courtney laughed. "Sounds like something I'd do." Then she sobered. "Tell me again which one of your relatives had money stolen?"

Melanie frowned, and her eyes burned with anger. "My godmother. She's nice. It makes me mad. Fortunately, she didn't lose a whole lot. My brother keeps up with her financial affairs and checks them regularly. With her blessing, of course. We both know there are lots of scammers out there. Our family tries to watch out for each other."

"So, she's okay financially?" Courtney hesitated before asking the question. People were sensitive about money.

"She's fine. She's wealthy, and Phil only got a little bit before my brother caught on to his shenanigans. Still, even if she can afford to lose it, obviously it's wrong. And look at all the hurt he caused these other people's relatives. I don't want anyone murdered, but I do wish he'd ended up in jail. And whatever anyone thinks about Kris, she's a savvy woman. I bet she knows exactly what Phil did with those investments. We've all learned Lauren fed her information, and Kris would have investigated Phil's dealings."

Courtney found the statement interesting. "Do you believe she killed her husband? She seemed upset yesterday, and today she appears genuinely depressed."

"You can kill someone you love because you feel you have a good reason, but still be sad they're gone," Melanie told her.

"Wow. Clarissa is going to have to be careful. You sound like a psychologist. She could lose her job here."

The frown lines dropped from Melanie's face, and she smiled at Courtney. "She doesn't need to worry."

"Anything else you can tell us?" Alex asked her.

"Not really." She took a drink of her water.

"Tell me about Skylar." Did she and Alex want to continue employing Skylar, since she had known about Phil and the guests? She added, "Only if you're okay with it though."

Melanie glanced at Courtney. "I guess I should have invited you both to my session with Dr. Alois. Though I didn't plan to confess I hid my gun under Jade's bed. Dr. Alois has such a calm, soothing way, I told her more than I intended."

They laughed. "Yes, Clarissa is one in a million."

Melanie relaxed against the back of the couch. "I'm not sure where to begin with the rest of the story."

Courtney patted her on the back. "Pretend you're telling Clarissa. We aren't going to tell anyone else what you tell us without checking with you first. It sounds like you're going to pass on the information about Jade and the gun. The information about Skylar can't be that damaging."

"No, it's not. I feel like I'm telling other people's secrets. People deserve their privacy." She wrapped her arms around her waist.

"Don't tell us anything you don't want to," Courtney said. "We'll find out some other way."

Melanie laughed. "Which almost sounds like a threat." She held up her hand before Courtney could respond. "I know you didn't mean it that way."

"I didn't," Courtney assured her.

"So, Skylar. She's struggling to make a life for herself. I don't believe it's a secret to you. She probably told you she needed the job to support her two kids, and her mom living in Elm City was a wonderful coincidence."

"Yes, she did. How was Hank related to Skylar?" Alex sat in the armchair with one leg crossed over the other and his ankle on his knee.

"It's complicated. Lucy is Skylar's mother. Hank was Lucy's husband's brother. Skylar kind of adopted Hank as a second father. Her own father left her mother and disappeared."

"And how is Jade related to Hank?"

"Hank was Jade's mother's brother. Her father died of cancer when she was a child. Hank was a safe place to go when she needed someone. From everything I've heard from Skylar and Jade, Hank was one of those kind and generous men.

"Skylar's situation mirrored Jade's, with Hank a replacement father figure for them. And then he lost all his money to Phil and couldn't handle the shame."

"That is sad."

They all sat there and pondered the situation.

Finally, Courtney got up and went to the fridge. "I hope Skylar isn't the killer. She's suffered enough. As has her mother. I can't imagine what Lucy would do if Skylar were guilty."

"Or Jade," Melanie said. "I'm leaning toward Lauren and Kris." She gasped and put her hand over her mouth, then dropped it. "I shouldn't have said it out loud."

Courtney pulled some salad out of the fridge, pretending not to be paying too much attention to Melanie's latest statement, but her mind was racing. During the last half hour, she'd found Melanie perceptive about people.

"Anyone else want something to eat? I'm starving," Courtney said.

Melanie looked at Alex.

"You're invited to eat with us." He smiled. "I know this is a strange situation. At some point, we're going to have to sneak you down to your room and pretend you were there all this time. Since Clarissa is telling everyone you're eating in your room, you may as well eat with us."

"I'd love to eat with you then," Melanie said. "I'm suddenly starving. It's all that confessing to Dr. Alois and then to the two of you. I haven't eaten much since Phil died because of the guilt I've felt about everything I knew and didn't tell anyone. I didn't know what to do."

"Glad you can share the information with us and feel better," Alex said. "Someday, when this is all over and you can get away for a vacation again, you're invited for a free week for the help you've given us."

She smiled wryly. "Two things about that invitation. I have a daughter, Sylvia. She'll have to come along."

"She's welcome," Alex assured her. "We'll have the backyard done by then, and she'll have plenty of space to play. And the second thing?"

"You want me to tell you about Kris and Lauren." She grimaced.

"The free week is not contingent on that. You get the free week no matter what. Telling us about Kris and Lauren is your choice. We're going to eat now, and you can decide while we're eating if

you want to say anything. We'll talk about
something else until we're finished."

CHAPTER 45

Melanie agreed to tell Courtney and Alex what she knew about Kris and Lauren. The three of them settled on the couch and armchair again, sitting where they sat before eating.

"First, I was kind of a mole in the whole group thing. I told my relative in law enforcement about what was going on, and he suggested I keep an eye on everyone. I didn't want to be there, but we both thought it was safe enough. We always met in public, and no one seemed homicidal." She made a face.

"What was your connection to Phil? Which relative?" Alex asked.

"It was my godmother, Harriet. She's sweet."

Courtney reached over and patted her hand. "Sounds tough."

"Well, only a few of us know what happened. She was embarrassed, as all victims of financial fraud are, and she didn't want to be known in the family as the one who fell for a scam. She has plenty of money, but as I told Dr. Alois, that doesn't matter. Her husband died a few years ago." Her fists clenched. "I've been visiting her as often as I can, and so have others in the family. I don't think she's caught on to us yet. We visited her quite often before this all happened anyway."

"That's nice of you," Alex said. "It balances out the evil of the world."

"It's the right thing to do." She said it like she couldn't imagine anyone else walking away from their relative when they were in distress.

"Well, good for you." Courtney took a sip of her soda. "So, you were watching out for what would happen in the group."

"And to see if there was any way we could get the money back for our relatives and Rory and Ivy. I was sorry for them. They worked hard for the downpayment on a house. Ivy was crushed, and Rory felt like a fool, although he put on an act of bravado, pretending he had suspicions all along."

"Ivy and Rory had the easiest opportunity to kill Phil. They were the last to see him alive," Alex said.

"I thought about that, but I can't see Rory killing someone with Ivy watching. She seems too soft-hearted."

Courtney shared a glance with Alex. A lot of soft-hearted people did bad things when forced into a corner.

"You wanted to know about Kris and Lauren." She frowned, and her fingers clenched together again. "I don't know what to tell you about Lauren. She appeared upfront and ready to share her opinion when we were together. She claimed it was her aunt who had been scammed."

"What was her opinion on the police investigation?" Courtney asked.

"We should push the police to move faster. She wanted Phil arrested. The strange thing is she never told us Phil was her uncle and Kris her aunt. So, essentially, her Uncle Phil scammed her, and she kept quiet. Or Phil and Kris did it together. What a mixed-up family."

"You think Kris knew what was going on?" Alex folded one leg over the other and tapped on his ankle.

"Definitely. At the beginning of this week, I would have said no, but I've seen too much of her and Lauren together in the last few days to believe Kris was in the dark as to where Phil got his money." She reached over to the coffee table and picked up her soda. After taking a long swallow, she set it back down and sighed. "I've seen more of the bad side of life in the past three days than I have in all the years before, and that's saying something."

Courtney got the feeling Melanie had a story to tell, and it wasn't a happy story. "So, what did you hear that concerned you?"

"Lauren asked Kris if she would have enough money to live on, since she was sure the police froze all of Phil and Kris's assets when he was murdered. Lauren said the police had been investigating Phil for a while, which was likely.

"Kris said she'd been putting some money away. She'd planned to divorce Phil and wanted to be prepared. I overheard her tell Lauren not to tell the police."

"The police don't know she was considering divorce or hid money?" Courtney found that unbelievable.

"I don't know. Maybe the police found out some other way," Melanie said. "If they investigated Phil for the last month, they might know more. Although these are the first search warrants they've served. Lauren would have told us if the detectives did a search before the murder, even though she didn't tell us her relationship to Kris and Phil. Kris seemed surprised and upset about the search warrant here. I'm sure she expected them to search in Minot at some point."

"How can you be sure Lauren would have told you about a search if she kept her relationship to Kris and Phil from you?" Alex asked.

Courtney was saddened by the bitterness in Alex's voice. Since they'd been building and preparing for the retreat, he'd been too busy to think about the past. For the most part, he'd accepted everything that happened, but he wouldn't be human if it didn't occasionally grate on him. He'd found God and prayed a lot.

She'd have to ask him this evening if he was getting in his prayer time. She'd slipped a lot since their guests arrived. And now was when she needed God's help the most.

"A search warrant would be public news, and even if we didn't know of her relationship with them, she'd want us to hear it from her, so she could put her own spin on it." Her bitter tone echoed Alex's expression.

"What about Braden? I thought he was working with Lauren. Wouldn't you expect to hear from him?" Alex tapped his fingers on his ankle where it was crossed on his other knee.

"I don't know how to explain it properly. When we started the group, Braden was in charge.

Gradually, Lauren took over." She stopped for a moment. "I never realized it before, but she became the driving force, and Braden let her. He might not have noticed. She was subtle with him. In fact, I hadn't considered it myself until now."

"Why do you think she was taking over? Wouldn't it have been better for her to fade into the background?"

"It's not her personality. I knew she was assertive, but I'm starting to believe she's manipulative too." Melanie leaned back against the sofa and sighed. "I'm tired of these people."

She laughed at herself. "I should have stopped meeting with them and let it all go. I guess I had this idea I was righting a wrong for a lot of older people Phil scammed. I felt part of something big."

Courtney smiled at her. "I'd say you were trying to do the right thing."

"Yes, but now I'm in the middle of a murder investigation." She swallowed the rest of her soda, holding the glass in her hand.

"The police know you were with Dr. Alois when Phil died. I think you're safe from arrest."

"I may have an alibi, but they're not going to like the facts I withheld about the gun in Jade's room."

"Take it moment by moment." Alex stood up. "It's time for you to quit thinking about this."

At her snort of a laugh, he said, "Well, as much as you can. We need to sneak you back down to your room."

"Good. I'll be happy to sit there all night with no interruptions or police presence." She stopped speaking for a moment. "Well, maybe I should be afraid to be alone."

"Braden and I are taking turns guarding the hallway tonight," Alex said. "I hope it helps you. Braden is innocent."

"Yes, it does make me feel better." She followed them down the stairs, and they stood by the door into the hallway.

"I'll go first and see if anyone can see us," Alex said. "Get your keycard for your room ready."

She pulled it out of her pocket and waited while he stepped into the hallway. He was back a second later. "All clear. Hold the door open, Courtney."

***

He and Melanie slipped quietly down the hallway, and he shielded her as she opened the door and slid into her room. The door closed at the same time Kris stepped out of her room.

"What's going on?" she asked. "I heard a door close."

"I was checking on Melanie. She's doing better but said she'll stay in her room for the rest of the night."

"Good. I'm glad she's okay." Kris dragged her dressing gown around herself. It was only seven in the evening, but she seemed ready for bed.

"How are you doing?" Alex asked her sympathetically.

Her eyes flicked closed and then opened. "I'm okay. Glad the police are gone. Although I don't feel as safe, I'm not afraid of being arrested. I didn't like the way they eyed me before they left." She shivered and pulled her dressing gown even tighter around herself.

"Please let me know if there's anything we can do for you. As I told Melanie, Braden and I will guard the hall tonight, so you know you're safe."

"Good. Thanks for letting me use Jade's room." She nodded, turned back into her room, and closed the door.

He heard the stairway door close, and Courtney came around the corner, joining him as he walked the hallway to the great room. "What next?" he asked.

"See what's up with the rest of our guests and maybe see if I can talk to any of them."

"Kris has holed up in her room for the night."

Courtney nodded. "That should be helpful. I'm going to stop in the kitchen and talk to Willow. Should you follow her home again tonight?"

"Yes. You okay being alone?" He knew she'd say yes, and he'd worry anyway.

"Sure. I'll keep Braden near me."

"We're putting a lot of faith in him," Alex said.

She stopped him and hugged him. "Our faith in him is not misplaced. You didn't make a mistake hiring him." She gave him a final squeeze and let go. She went into the kitchen to talk to Willow.

CHAPTER 46

The great room was empty when Courtney joined Alex by the fridge. He pulled out a bottle of water.

"Willow's accepted your offer to follow her home and is ready to leave when you are. Let's have Skylar help her all morning, and Willow can leave right after lunch tomorrow. She's put in some long days. We'll figure out the evening meal."

"Okay. I'll go tell her I'm ready. Lauren and Braden are watching some movie." He gestured toward the television room and left to get Willow. "Everyone else seems to be in their rooms."

Courtney looked in at the two people sitting on a black leather couch facing the television. "Anything good?"

"An old movie," Braden answered. "Want to join us?"

"Sure." She sat in the armchair angled to see the TV screen. She felt eyes on her but didn't know who was watching. She turned quickly and caught Lauren's gaze. She smiled at her.

"How are you doing?" Courtney asked her.

"Fine. Aunt Kris settled down finally. I don't know what she's going to do when she gets home."

"Does she have siblings she can turn to?"

"They've mostly written her off. She can be kind of snobbish and has a prickly personality. Not many people want to spend time in her company."

Lauren shrugged. "It's hard though. Uncle Phil loved her in his own way. Sometimes I think he thought she'd leave him if he didn't provide her with endless amounts of money."

"That's sad. Who knows what will happen now? I guess time will tell if she's implicated in his scams or not." Courtney didn't feel the need to pull her punches with Lauren. She hardly seemed the bereaved niece regarding Phil. "So, what was your plan for this week?"

Lauren tensed slightly. "What do you mean?" She glanced at the television.

"You may as well mute it," she said to Braden, who held the remote and watched them.

He pushed the mute button, and the room went silent.

"What was the plan for this whole week and getting everyone here?" Courtney asked Lauren. "What were you going to accomplish?"

Lauren looked at Braden, who shrugged and said, "I already told her we wanted to get the money back for our relatives, and we didn't send the blackmail text in the first place."

"But you took advantage of the situation. How did you plan to get the money back, Lauren? Yes, I'm asking you," she said when Lauren glanced at Braden again.

Lauren's gaze returned to her. Only a twitch by the corner of her mouth indicated emotion at the question. "We were going to harass him."

"Exactly what would that consist of?" Courtney suddenly realized she might be questioning two people who conspired to kill Phil, putting herself in danger. She pushed the thought away. Too late now. And they had decided Braden wasn't part of the murder.

"Anonymous calls. Nasty notes. Things like that." Lauren shifted into a more comfortable position on the couch.

"Couldn't you have done those things when he was in Minot? Why lure him out here?" That angered her the most. Her dream inn, and they were using it to harass someone.

"Like Braden said, we didn't know he was going to come out here at first. Kris told me." If Lauren was lying, she did it well.

Braden nodded. "It was a complete surprise to us. I wouldn't have lured him to where I work. I have more integrity." He sounded as aggrieved as Courtney felt.

"I didn't want him anywhere near me. The plan to harass him didn't start until he got the text to come out here and meet someone. And I have no idea who suggested the idea either. Suddenly it was being whispered around the table. Kind of like the old game Telephone. It spreads, and by the time it gets to the last person in the circle, the meaning is totally different from the starting words."

"And neither of you know who sent him the text?" Courtney didn't buy they didn't know. Lauren could have sent it.

"No way. We wanted him at home," Lauren said. "It was easier. As you can see, now we're all sitting ducks in the police suspect pool. That's no way to plot a murder."

Courtney shivered at her words. Had she thought of plotting her uncle's death a different way? "Well, someone did. Any idea who? You both spent a lot of time meeting with these people."

"I can guess who it wasn't," Lauren said. "Ivy and Melanie. Melanie's been in her room all day today. That's not someone who can plan a game like this. Ivy follows Rory, but she's sweet. I can't see it."

"Sometimes it's the people you wouldn't expect it to be," Braden said. "Not that I'm disagreeing about those two. I doubt it was either of them. But look at Jade. I wouldn't have thought she'd bring a gun and threaten Phil. He could have grabbed the gun easily and shot her."

"Yes. She got lucky, because I'm betting he was surprised she had so much anger in her. Like we were surprised. Although," she turned to Braden, "do you remember when Kris was going around offering money to our relatives to keep them quiet?"

Braden sat up from his slouch. "Jade raved on and on about revenge, but she wears out fast. She's like a firecracker. One boom, and then it's over."

Courtney straightened and leaned forward. "If Kris offered money to people Phil defrauded, who did she offer money to for Hank, since he was dead? Was it Jade?"

"No. She talked to Skylar's mom, Lucy," Braden said. "Skylar said Lucy told Kris to get out of her house and never come back. She didn't need her money. It was blood money for Hank. We tried to get the money back for Lauren's aunt, but Kris refused."

He looked at Lauren. "I guess it was your money, not your aunt's. Which is why she wouldn't give it back."

"The only other one we know she offered money to was Rory," Lauren told her.

Braden looked at Courtney where she sat listening. "Rory accepted. He said he wanted it all, everything he lost, or he would report Phil. She said she'd get it to him later."

Which sounded like Rory. Courtney remembered he wanted a refund for the week at the inn. "You know, it seems to me Kris's motive would be to kill one of you. You went after her and Phil. If you left them alone, your older relatives wouldn't go after them. Am I right?"

"Right," Braden agreed. "Most of them were too embarrassed by the whole situation."

"Well, there's no way Aunt Kris would send us a letter and then kill us here. She'd be the prime suspect."

"But why would she kill Phil? What does it gain her in the end? His death is going to be public news, and so are the scams he perpetrated," Courtney said. "She'd be better off convincing him to move somewhere else and start over."

"Kind of makes it look like someone else killed him, doesn't it?" Lauren said hopefully. "I don't like to think she killed him."

For the first time since Courtney met her, Lauren appeared vulnerable. Phil and Kris were her relatives. Maybe the tough act was from something that happened and not a personality trait.

She changed the subject. "Did Rory get any money back?"

Braden shook his head. "Not a cent. We didn't expect him to, but Rory had hopes."

"Sounds like a strong motive, although killing Phil wasn't going to get him his money back either."

"No, but it would be revenge, and sometimes Rory can have a tantrum like a two-year-old. I'm not saying he's guilty," Braden hastily added. "I'm not accusing anyone, because I have no idea."

Courtney looked at Lauren. "Any guesses?"

Lauren grimaced. "A few, but I'm not comfortable sharing. I have no proof, and I could be wrong."

Courtney nodded. "I understand why you wouldn't want to accuse the wrong person."

"How about you?" Lauren's voice held a dare.

"No idea. I can rule a few people out of pulling the trigger. I saw Braden off and on all afternoon. Willow was stuck in the kitchen. Melanie was seen by enough people here to have an alibi. Neither Hugh nor Clarissa had any free time or any reason. I was here all afternoon, and I know Alex wouldn't want any bad publicity, nor did he know what was going on until Phil was killed."

"Which leaves a few of us. Me included," Lauren said thoughtfully. "I wonder if I can figure it out."

"Oh no. Leave the investigation to the professionals. The person killed someone. Don't give them a reason to come after you," Courtney said.

"Like *you* are leaving it to the professionals?" Lauren called her bluff.

"Right," she said firmly. The front door opened, and she got up and looked out the television room doorway to see who it was. Alex had returned. She turned back to Lauren and Braden. "Do you know if Rory and Ivy are here now?"

"No. They went out and said they would be late. They went to Dickinson to party," Braden said.

"Okay. I'm going to bed. Braden, you get first watch tonight until 1:00 a.m. Then Alex will take over. Sit where the deputy did to see any movement of people between rooms. We need to keep everyone safe, at least here in the building, until they leave. I'm giving you the benefit of the doubt and trusting you."

"Got it." He didn't seem to mind watching the others. "Thank you for trusting me."

"Text if there's a problem."

"Okay."

"Good night." She left them to follow Alex up to their apartment. They didn't discuss anything until they settled in the living room, snuggled up on the couch together.

Courtney had showered and changed into her pajamas, and Alex had too. "I got some new information from Braden and Lauren tonight."

"I want to hear, but first let's make a pact. We discuss it all right now, then we relax before bed for a while. A movie, a book, some prayers," he said.

"Sure. My mind needs a break, and I have gotten lax in talking to God."

He laughed. "He'll let us know in His own time, but we should thank Him no one else has been hurt. And ask for guidance to find the right answer. Whether it's the police or us who finds the answer doesn't matter. Let's get these guests home safely and start doing more for the wedding."

"You're right." She knew Alex was better at constant prayer than her. "Okay. It's a deal. So, Braden and Lauren told me Kris went around to some of the people who were scammed and offered to return their money. They all felt insulted by the move, from what Braden and Lauren told me tonight. Skylar's mom got particularly nasty, according to what Skylar told the others."

"Money for Hank's life." His eyes held a sadness she'd seen only a few times. Man's inhumane treatment of others. He had such a soft heart.

"Yes," she said softly. "Even I might get hostile toward someone who offered me money in those circumstances. Like it would bring Hank back." She shook her head.

He took her hand in his. "How did I get so lucky marrying you?"

"You're a good man. You deserve the best," she teased.

He didn't smile but pulled her closer. "You are the best. The best thing that ever happened to me. After God, of course."

"Of course." She hid her face in his pajama top, inhaling his soapy scent. "You are the best thing that ever happened to me too."

"We're lucky."

"I've missed you these past few days," she said.

"Too much going on. Hang in there. Two more days, and they're all gone."

She sighed. "When the guests leave, we're going to have to talk to Skylar and Braden. They've abused our trust. I don't know if we can continue employing them."

"I know," Alex sighed too. "Let's talk about something else tonight."

"Agreed. I thought of something when I was talking to Lauren. Why would she or Kris send a blackmail text to Phil saying they would contact the police if he didn't come to the inn? They knew Phil was aware the police were already investigating. A blackmail text like that wouldn't accomplish what they wanted, which was to get him here."

"And yet, he came," Alex said.

"Because Kris convinced him to come. Maybe she used the argument they needed to know who sent the text. They were doing their own investigating into the group investigating them."

"My head's beginning to whirl." Alex put his hand on her shoulder, and his eyes met hers. "I give up for tonight. I can't think anymore. How about you?"

"Totally understand. My mind needs to stop and let the subconscious take over for the night."

"Good." He kissed her nose, and she snuggled back into his shoulder.

Two days to figure out what was going on. She finally had an idea and didn't like it one bit. "Let's forget about it for the rest of the night. You have to replace Braden for guard duty at 1:00 a.m. You should get some sleep."

She stuffed down her anger whenever she thought about the situation. She prayed God would take her anger away. He could do that.

She needed to accept their first week of the opening had been a disaster. Only God could make sure it didn't affect their rating, and people wanted to stay at the inn. She needed to remember, even though Phil had done a lot of bad things, he was a human being who didn't deserve to be killed.

CHAPTER 47
Wednesday Morning

The night passed peacefully, and when Alex returned to their room at 6:00 a.m., Courtney got ready for the day. She took time to say her prayers, knowing she needed lots of spiritual intervention to get through the day.

Alex went back to bed, and she promised to wake him at ten. Then she left him to join Willow in the kitchen. Yesterday, she'd texted Skylar and told her she'd be doing kitchen duty instead of housekeeping.

She left Willow for a few minutes to see if anyone else was moving, but everyone was in their rooms. Their vehicles were all in the parking lot, including Rory and Ivy's SUV. She was glad to see they'd returned safely. She didn't know if they were heavy drinkers or only liked to socialize, but they'd made it back, which was all that mattered.

She cooked with Willow until Skylar arrived, and then she left them to the rest of the preparations. Willow whistled at being able to leave right after lunch.

"Alex and I can oversee the evening meal with Skylar. We'll make sandwiches and a salad or two. There are some leftover desserts, which should be good enough."

"Is your mother taking care of the kids today?" Courtney asked Skylar after she okayed the plan.

"Yes, she is." Skylar peeled potatoes by the sink, letting the peels fall into the garbage can in front of her.

"Is she okay with you working full days this week? Or should we make other plans?"

Skylar's lips turned up, and she looked young. "She loves the kids. In fact, if you decide you need more hours from me, she'd be quite happy to continue spoiling them when I'm not around, and I could use the money."

"That's good." Courtney let the thought of her coming conversation with Skylar and Braden slip from her mind. One thing at a time.

She plotted her morning. As soon as Alex got up, she would be visiting Lucy's neighbor and then Lucy. She wanted to hear more about Kris's offer to replace the money Phil scammed from Hank.

"Our neighbor across the street watches the children sometimes." Skylar looked up, a question in her eyes.

"You told me." Courtney forced out a smile. "What's her name?"

"I call her Mrs. B. Her name is Beatrice Hamilton. She was a grade-school teacher and didn't believe in being too strict. She's a marshmallow; although, when I was a child, I didn't see her that way." She started rinsing off the potatoes in the sink and adding them to a bowl. "What next?" she asked Willow.

"How about grating some cheese, dicing some tomatoes, and shredding the lettuce?" Willow answered as she stirred some ground hamburger on the stove.

"We're making taco fixings for you for this evening," she told Courtney. "Should make it easier for you and Alex."

"You're both angels!" Courtney hugged them each gently, keeping clear of knives and hot stoves. "I'm leaving you to it while I gather the troops for breakfast, if you're ready."

"We are," they said in unison.

After the guests' breakfast, Courtney took a tray up to Alex. She found him sitting in the armchair reading his Bible.

"Food," she said as she entered.

"Yeah, I'm starving." Before their meal, they prayed.

"What are doing today?" Alex asked.

"I'm running into town for an errand right now. I'm going to see Lucy about Kris before Skylar gets home. I want a first-hand account of what happened when Kris offered her money. I also want to talk to the neighbor across the street. Skylar calls her Mrs. B. She watches the children sometimes if Lucy and Skylar need a babysitter. I'm guessing they ask her so she feels useful. She used to be a schoolteacher."

"Maybe she'd prefer not to babysit after retiring from a school," Alex said.

"Maybe. Or she could be lonely, and they're what she needs. I'll see," she said. "How about you? What's your plan?"

"Move my laptop to the kitchen and keep an eye out for everyone while I work."

"Sounds good. I should be back by lunch at the latest. Neither visit will take very long."

"You never know," Alex said. "You'll be offered cookies and something to drink."

She laughed. "You're right. I shouldn't have eaten so much at breakfast, but Willow is such a great cook."

CHAPTER 48

Courtney pulled up to Mrs. B's home. The buttercup-yellow house had nicely trimmed shrubs on either side of the front steps and a freshly raked lawn. She thought about the amount of work the inn needed before the wedding in two weeks and shuddered. Maybe Mrs. B would like a challenge. Or if a relative did the work—maybe they could use some extra money.

She went up the walkway, and, as she reached the bottom step, the front door opened. "Hello." She looked up at the woman in the doorway. "I'm looking for Mrs. B. Am I at the right house? Skylar said she lives across the street."

"I'm Mrs. B." She was a silver-haired woman with a lovely soft face and cushiony body. She looked like she'd made an excellent, sweet teacher for young children. She leaned on a cane. Obviously, she wasn't the one keeping the yard immaculate.

"Hello. I'm Courtney Richmond. Skylar works for me at the new Crocus Hill Inn outside of town."

"I've seen you at the store a few times," Mrs. B. said.

"Do you have a moment to talk? I have a question about a visitor Lucy and Skylar had one day. I'm concerned about them. Plus, I'd like to talk to Lucy alone, and I was wondering if you would watch the children while I talk to her?"

When Mrs. B didn't say anything, Courtney continued her plea. "Please? I guess I should have known you'd be hesitant to talk about your neighbors, but you don't have to answer any questions. If I could at least ask them, you could decide whether you want to answer or not."

She waited while Mrs. B studied her.

"Come on in." Mrs. B held the door open for her as she walked up the steps and into the house.

Courtney stood aside as Mrs. B closed the door and then followed her into the room. The front door opened right into the living room.

"Have a chair."

Courtney sat down in the nearest armchair. The room was decorated in a sparse fashion, but a few treasured knickknacks were placed on top of a bookshelf.

Mrs. B took up a position on a hard-backed chair across from her. She hadn't offered any refreshments yet. "So, what can I tell you?"

Right to the point. Must be the steel under the soft exterior to keep the kids in line. "Lucy had a visitor about a month ago. A woman with short dark brown hair. Since she came to the inn, she's worn jeans every day and usually a soft plaid button-down shirt."

"I know exactly who you mean. Kris Young." She chuckled at Courtney's stunned expression. "The grapevine in a small town is active. Have you ever lived in a small town?"

"For a few years." She had a passing thought of Chokecherry Valley. "Very similar in size to Elm City, so, yes, I know how fast news travels."

"When they showed the picture of Phil Young and his wife on the internet, I recognized her. She did come to visit Lucy about a month ago."

"Did Lucy say they were friends?" Courtney asked.

"No." Mrs. B frowned. "In fact, I have never seen her so mad, except when Hank killed himself. Except, with Hank's death, there was a lot of sadness. This anger was pure hate." She pulled her dark cardigan closer around her, as if suddenly chilled.

She went on, "For Kris to offer her the money Hank lost to her husband is the most insulting thing I've ever heard of. And I've heard of a lot of bad things. Yes, even in a small town. Especially in a small town. Everybody is in everybody else's business, and they choose sides. The best thing to do in a small town is stay out of any arguments, unless it's going to harm someone."

Courtney's heart sank at the words. She needed Mrs. B's help.

"I need to interfere now though." Mrs. B surprised her by these words. "I saw Kris Young at Lucy's the day Phil was killed."

Courtney straightened in her chair, stunned at the announcement. "Let me think for a minute."

She thought back to the day when Kris wandered the town during her wait for Phil. She stopped by sometime during that afternoon, and Lucy and Skylar were home. Except for the time

Lucy went to the grocery store. "Do you know what time she stopped by to talk to Lucy or Skylar?"

"It was a little after two o'clock, and my favorite afternoon show was on, so I didn't pay a lot of attention. I thought it strange. Kris appeared to slip into the side door of the garage. The one you can't see from the front of the house. I thought that because she disappeared around the corner, and then I didn't see her until she came back out the front door. She came out within ten minutes, and even from here, I could see how red her face was. She looked furious.

"Then Lucy left about ten minutes later and went to the grocery store. At least that's what Skylar told me later. Something about being short of chocolate chips, which I thought was funny, because Lucy loves her chocolate. I can't see her running out of that ingredient. Maybe something else, but not chocolate."

Courtney was getting a bad feeling. "Listen, Mrs. B, you don't know me, so you don't have to believe what I'm going to say. I'm not even sure I'm right. Would you mind if the children stayed with you for a while? I need to talk to Lucy. It could be dangerous."

Mrs. B. shook her head. "Then you should leave Lucy alone."

"I can't do that. It's not right. There are a bunch of guests at my inn who are going to be murder suspects for the rest of their lives if this crime isn't solved."

Mrs. B. studied her and then nodded. "And you've solved it."

Courtney nodded. "I need to call the sheriff, and even if he doesn't believe me, I'm going to tell him. Do you have his number?"

"Okay." She got up from her seat briskly. "I guess we have to do the right thing. I'll go tell Lucy I want to see the kids and feed them lunch. She'll appreciate the break. Until you get there." Her face was full of sadness.

"I know."

She rummaged through her things on a desk in the corner and pulled out a much-used old-fashioned address book. "Here's the sheriff's number."

As she rattled it off, Courtney programmed it into her phone. She should have brought along the detective's card from Minot, but that could wait. She sent a quick text message to Alex about what was happening.

She left Mrs. B. sitting there, staring across the street with her lips quivering. She would cry later.

When Courtney closed the front door behind her, her phone rang. Alex. She answered as she crossed the street.

During the walk, Alex made his thoughts known. "You have got to be kidding me," he shouted in her ear. "Do not go over there."

"She's not going to do anything to me," she reassured him. "I'm going to ask her if Kris had some way to get out to Phil's location. I'm calling the sheriff now."

CHAPTER 49

When she hung up from talking to Alex and let the sheriff know Lucy saw Kris the day of the murder, she stood there waiting for Mrs. B to call Lucy. All too soon, Lucy's front door opened, and she came outside with the two children.

Kyle grinned his gap-toothed smile at her. "I know you. You visited Nanna before. I showed you my picture."

"I remember." She smiled back at him. "It was a very nice picture. So, you get to visit Mrs. B while I visit your Nanna."

"That's what Mrs. B said." He held a stuffed backpack in front of him. "I have my toys in here. Want to see them?"

"Can I see them when I come back? I'm going to visit your Nanna, and then I'll look."

"Okay," he agreed.

Courtney looked up and said hello to Lucy.

She returned the greeting with a resigned look on her face. "I'll get the children settled at Mrs. B's house."

Courtney followed, watching her shepherd the kids up to Mrs. B's door. Violet clung to Mrs. B as soon as she opened the door. Lucy left after a subdued smile and thank you.

"I'll be back in a while," Courtney said to Mrs. B. "I don't know how long this will take. My husband, Alex, might be rushing here now, so if you see him, you'll know." She left the safety of the house and headed across the street to see Lucy.

CHAPTER 50

Lucy stood at the door waiting for Courtney to cross the street. When she climbed the stairs, Lucy held the door open.

Courtney walked into the living room and stood waiting for Lucy to sit down. Again, she wasn't offered any refreshments. Lucy finally sat down in a chair by the couch, and Courtney perched on the arm of the couch.

"Mrs. B. told me you wanted to talk to me. Is there something wrong with Skylar?"

Courtney realized it was an opening question. If there had been something wrong with her daughter, she wouldn't have been calm, and Skylar would have texted her.

"No. This isn't about Skylar. It's about you and Kris." She heard the quick intake of breath Lucy stifled.

"Kris and I?" she scoffed. "Sworn enemies. She should be dead along with Phil for what they did." Her voice rose at the end. "I had my chance and didn't take it."

Courtney's hand froze on the way to help her keep her balance on the couch, and she plopped onto the cushion. "What are you talking about? Didn't Kris come about a month ago to offer you money?"

Lucy stood up and started pacing. She glared at the floor, remembering. "She stopped by one day. I sent Skylar and the kids into the other room and told Kris what I thought of her offer. Not that sending the others to another room made any difference. I screamed so loud, Mrs. B probably heard me across the street. Anyway, she didn't stay when she realized there was no way I was taking a payoff to forget about what happened to Hank and the others."

"Why did she come back on Monday? Mrs. B saw her come out of your house. She wasn't sure how she got in, but I assume that door connects to another entrance." She pointed to a door farther into the room where a rug lay with a few small sneakers scattered on top of it.

"I didn't see her. I didn't know she came back," Lucy denied the charge.

"I'm sure you did. Mrs. B saw you leave the house about ten minutes after Kris. She also saw Kris leave by the front door with a furious look on her face. I could also ask Skylar what happened." Courtney wasn't sure what Lucy's next statement would be, but she thought the woman had lied about a lot of things.

"I went to the store. Maybe Kris came when I was already gone, and Skylar didn't tell me about it. She knows how that woman makes my blood boil." She sat down on a rocker across the room.

"You accepted money from her last time, didn't you? She threatened to tell the others you did. Am I right?" Courtney asked.

"Okay. She owed Hank money, and if I could use it for Skylar and the kids, I thought it wouldn't hurt. I was wrong. The minute she left, I knew, if she came back, I'd throw it in her face." Lucy rocked furiously.

"But she didn't come back until Monday. And why did she do that?" Courtney was aware of the outside door opening, and suddenly the room held Alex, Skylar, and Kris. Alex wouldn't have brought them with him. Had they followed him, sensing something was wrong?

Lucy stared right at Kris. "She wanted me to take her out to the gun range where Phil was practicing. She told me she'd been walking around town long enough and was ready to go back to the inn. I guess she thought I'd help her, since I was the only person she knew in town.

"At first I refused to take her. Why would I? She'd made my life hell, and I wasn't doing her any favors. She told me she was going to kill Phil. She'd sent him a text a month or so ago to come to the inn. Said she'd threatened him. Then she convinced him to come out here and find out who the sender was. She said she planned it all out so there would be plenty of suspects, and she'd be one of many.

"That day, she needed a ride and knew I hated him enough to give her one. She snuck into the back of my car while it was in the garage, so no one would see her. Then we went out to where Phil waited, because she texted him to meet her out there, and she killed him."

Kris strode forward and stood right in front of Lucy. "You liar. I did not send him a text to meet, and I did not get a ride from you to go kill my husband. You went by yourself after I left here. How else would you know he received the anonymous text that brought him to the inn in the first place?"

"That's not what I'm going to tell the police. I was there. I saw you."

Courtney turned to Skylar. "Are you sure you want to be here?"

Tears filled Skylar's eyes. "I have to know what happened. I was afraid of this."

"You're very courageous." Courtney saw Sheriff Warren slip in behind Skylar before she turned back to Lucy and Kris. "Kris, I suggest you back up before Lucy attacks you."

Kris took a closer look at Lucy and moved away to stand by the window facing the street. Courtney saw Kris's relieved expression when she noticed the sheriff.

"Kris is right," Courtney said gently. "You killed Phil. Didn't you, Lucy? You sent the anonymous text so Phil would come stay at the inn. You wanted everyone in Skylar's group to be suspects. You didn't think the police would focus on anyone specific because they all had motive, but there'd be no proof against any of them." She sent Skylar a sympathetic look.

"Mom!" Skylar ran over to her mother, who rocked faster and faster, as if trying to outrun her actions. Skylar stopped the rocker and leaned down to look at her mother's face. "Tell me you didn't do what she said. Tell me now." Her voice rose urgently.

Lucy's gaze dropped from her daughter's expression. "I did, honey. I can't keep it in any longer. I did take money from Kris the first time. Then, when she came by Monday, the moment had come to take care of Phil. I didn't run out of chocolate chips. I hid them in the back of the cupboard and used it as an excuse.

"When Kris left, I texted Phil another anonymous text, and I stopped at the grocery store to provide the alibi. I didn't realize Kris would be at the grocery store wasting time until Phil picked her up. I kept avoiding her."

"I noticed you didn't buy anything," Kris said.

"I left without anything. I didn't need anything except to get out to where I agreed to meet Phil. He didn't know who he was meeting, but he was curious. He laughed when he saw me."

Indignation colored her voice. "He wasn't afraid of me, a middle-aged woman. He should have remembered Jade's actions. She couldn't shoot him, but I could." There was a note of satisfaction in her voice. "I told him what I thought of him and how he treated Hank, so he would know exactly who I was. Then I shot him."

Skylar paled. "Mom?"

Courtney stood up and put a hand on Skylar's arm. "It's time your mom quits talking and gets a lawyer."

"Oh, I don't care about going to jail. I deserve it," Lucy said.

The sheriff jumped in and read her rights to her. "Ma'am, you're under arrest for the murder of Philip Young."

Lucy looked at Skylar. "I'm sorry. I used one of Uncle Hank's guns."

The sheriff nodded. "We ran it through the database, and it was registered under Hank Wilkinson. You were next of kin in his will."

Tears coursed down Skylar's face. "You should have gotten rid of them when he killed himself. Oh, why did you keep them? What am I going to do?"

Courtney put her arms around Skylar, while the sheriff led Lucy out of the room. She didn't resist at all. Alex came over and stood beside her as she comforted Skylar.

Even Kris's face lost color. Courtney hoped she finally realized what she'd done to this family and all the other families she and Phil scammed.

Skylar's tears slowed, and she sat in the rocker where her mother had been rocking moments before. She glanced around the room, looking lost. "Where are the kids?"

"Mrs. B has them," Courtney told her.

"I need to see them." Skylar stood up like an old woman. "I need to hold them."

"Okay. Why don't you go wash your face, and then we'll go over to Mrs. B's house?"

Skylar left the room, and Kris left the house.

Alex opened his arms, and Courtney slipped into them. "Why was Kris here?" she asked.

"She overheard my phone call with you and followed me. So did Skylar. I didn't have time to stop them when I saw them in my rearview mirror. What's next?"

"I'll take Skylar across the street, and you go back to the inn for the lunch crowd."

"What do we tell them?" Alex asked.

"Nothing. You can tell Willow you'll help her with lunch because Skylar had something come up with the kids."

"Won't Kris tell them?"

Courtney thought about Kris's expression when she left. "I get the feeling she's suddenly ashamed. I don't know though. I doubt if it will last. She might tell Lauren, and then it'll get around to the rest of the group."

"Let them spread the news. I'm not saying anything except to Hugh and Clarissa," he said.

"Me either."

"I might contact Nathan and see if he can find an attorney for Lucy. I think she's been under so much pressure, she's lost touch with reality."

"You're a good man, Mr. Richmond." She hugged him and let go. "Now go feed our guests, and I'll be home as soon as I'm done checking what I can do for Skylar."

CHAPTER 51

The guests were subdued that evening as they gathered in the great room with Courtney, Alex, Hugh, and Clarissa after a quiet dinner. Courtney told Clarissa, Hugh, and Willow of the afternoon's events already, but now she had gathered the guests to talk with them.

Her anger had subsided to a dull ache of regret. These young people wasted a week of their lives on revenge and their own anger.

She sat down in front of them where they'd gathered on the couches and armchairs in the biggest grouping of the room. Alex sat in the navy recliner where Phil started out his week—a solemn reminder life was unpredictable.

"I asked you all to join me for a short update on what has happened since Phil's death. Kris is in her room resting. We offer our sympathies to Lauren on the death of her uncle."

Lauren nodded at the murmurs around her. She'd no doubt pass on the conversation to her aunt, for which Courtney didn't blame her.

Rory and Ivy's subdued expressions were shared by Melanie, Lauren, and Braden. Of their seven guests, only four joined them now.

"I'll start with the main part and go backward. Skylar's mother, Lucy, took advantage of Skylar working here to get her revenge on Phil. She never forgave him for her brother-in-law's suicide. She blamed Hank's death on Phil scamming him.

"I believe, at the end, she lost all sense of reason and formed the plan you all became a part of. With Skylar working here, she had inside information on what was happening. She also learned of all of you wanting to seek revenge for your own or your relatives' losses.

"She sent the first blackmail text to Phil to get him to stay here. Once he was here, she used the burner phone to send him another message to meet her out by the gun range after he finished with Rory and Ivy. Without Skylar's knowledge, she pumped her own daughter for everyone's movements.

"There were enough of you who came to stay at the retreat, she knew there would be plenty of suspects." She noticed they were all avoiding each other's eyes and staring at her.

"For a brief time while the sheriff was there this afternoon, she accused Kris, but Kris had nothing to do with Phil's death. She loved him. Lucy hoped to blame Kris and get away with murdering Phil, but the truth came out.

"That's the story. You're all welcome to stay until Friday, as you've paid for the week. We'll refund the portion you paid for the A New Day program. You're welcome to meet with Clarissa or Hugh at any time, if you want to make an appointment. Thank you for listening. If you have any questions, let me know."

They sat there in silence, covertly glancing at each other. No one asked anything or said anything.

"Okay, then. If you want to ask in private, that's okay too. The rest of the week is yours to relax and enjoy your time here." She didn't want to stay in the room, so she left them sitting there. Alex caught up with her in the hallway as she opened the door to their office.

Once they were inside with the door closed, he took her in his arms. "You did a good job. Summed it up perfectly without blaming them for coming."

"I don't know if it would have made a difference if they had stayed away." She snuggled in his arms. "It's nice to have that over with. When they leave, we need to take a day and recuperate. I don't care if there's a wedding to prepare for in a few weeks."

He kissed the top of her head. "Good plan."

CHAPTER 52

Friday afternoon finally arrived, and all the guests left by noon. A few took sandwiches for the road. Courtney decided, in the future, they would only offer breakfast in the morning, and sandwiches and soup in the evening. Willow didn't have time for more. Or they'd have to hire additional help.

She sighed with relief and looked at Alex where they sat at the dining table in the great room, looking outside and enjoying the silence. "Well, that turned out to be an interesting week."

He laughed. "What an understatement. You want to sell this place?"

"No way." She'd thought all last night about the reason she'd opened the inn. She wanted to assist others, and she thought Melanie had been helped. As for the other guests, they weren't here for the right reasons, but she knew the week gave some of the group closure. Nothing was perfect.

Right now, she and Alex waited for Skylar to arrive with her children. Clarissa agreed to watch the kids while the adults discussed the situation.

Braden entered the room uncertainly and chose a chair across the table from them. "Hi."

"How's the work going?" Alex asked. Braden was getting closer to finishing the backyard landscaping.

"Pretty well." He took a deep breath and exhaled. "I'm sorry."

Alex nodded. "I know."

They heard the sound of a vehicle on gravel and looked up to see Skylar arrive. They sat in silence while she unloaded the kids and their toys. She helped them up the stairs and into the house.

Clarissa came into the room. After a few minutes of conversation with Skylar and her kids, they all went into the television room and closed the door. Soon Skylar came out and joined Alex, Courtney, and Braden at the table.

"How are you doing?" Courtney noted the dark circles under her eyes and her drooping face.

"Okay." Her voice was subdued. "Are you going to fire us?"

"That depends." Courtney and Alex agreed ahead of time she would guide the conversation, as it was her dream to keep Crocus Hill Inn open. He'd go with her wishes on staffing. "Alex and I are disappointed neither of you were open with us about the guests. You both broke our trust. We're talking with you both at the same time, so you know you're getting equal treatment.

"You lied to us, both by omission and by some of the things you said. To a certain extent, we can understand, but you're not children. There are consequences. You had an agenda and didn't consider how betraying us or how the reputation your actions have caused would impact the future of the inn."

She held up her hand when Braden opened his mouth. "I'm not finished. You had a chance to speak before all this happened, and you didn't. Maybe you don't trust Alex and me either. How can we progress from here when none of us trust each other? Yes, you can answer now."

Braden glanced at Skylar, who sat there quietly, slumped in her chair. "First, I'm sorry about your mom, Skylar."

"Thanks," she mumbled.

He looked at Alex and Courtney. "I'll answer for myself. I'd like to stay here and work. I know I made some bad decisions, and I should have told you both what was going on from the beginning. I guess I was afraid you would change your mind, since I'd been in jail, and then all these people came here. You know the jail term was for my third drinking while intoxicated charge, and I cleaned up my act.

"You're right. I didn't consider how this would affect you and only thought about myself and keeping the other guests' secrets. I can promise you, if you let me continue working here, I will keep you informed about anything concerning you, and I will keep all activities within the law.

"I know what you did for your friend, Alex. I guess I'm trying to say, I look up to you for taking the blame for your friend and going to prison for him. That took real love of your friend. Wanting your respect made me hide things I didn't think you'd approve of me doing," he said to Alex, sounding sincere.

"Alex doesn't expect you to 'live up' to him." Courtney looked at Alex.

"Definitely not. My situation was different. You can't compare my experience and your time in jail. We both made mistakes. Let's try not repeating them. We'll make new ones. I'm including all of us when I say we're not perfect," Alex said.

Braden nodded. "Okay."

Courtney looked at Skylar. "What do you want to say? Can you even continue working here when you need someone to watch the children?"

Skylar sat up straight and put her hands flat on the table. "I'm sorry for my part too. I never knew my mother killed Phil until the very end. In hindsight, I should have guessed, but it didn't occur to me. As far as not telling you the plan, you're right, and I'm sorry. It was a lousy thing to do. I felt stuck. I needed this job to take care of the kids, and I didn't believe you'd understand everyone coming here to get revenge."

"We wouldn't. We would have stopped the whole thing, and Phil might be alive. He may not have been the best man in the world, but he shouldn't have been murdered." Courtney looked at Alex again, and he nodded.

She turned back to Braden and Skylar. "You can consider working here under two conditions. Never lie to us again. And keep us updated on anything concerning the inn. The caveat is if something else like this happens, that's it. This is your last chance." She didn't want to fire them. Skylar faced a lot of grief with her mother's arrest, and Braden would have trouble getting another job as an ex-con. "Let's try and rebuild some trust between us."

Skylar breathed a sigh of relief, and Braden's face gained some color.

"Skylar, what are you doing about the children when you're working? If we don't have guests, they can be here, but sometimes that won't be possible."

"Mrs. B said she'd watch them. Also, Jade is going to come and live with me at Mom's house until the trial and everything is completed. She'll help me with the kids. I'll work it out."

"Okay. Then you're both still employed, if you want to continue working here?" she asked.

"I do." Braden looked away from them for a minute, then turned back. "I'd like to learn about the Bible and God from Hugh, if you think he'd be interested. I want to be a better person like you and Alex. I know I need help. Would Hugh be okay teaching me?"

A smile spread across Alex's face. "Of course he would. Go ahead and work it out with him."

Braden smiled back at Alex. "Thank you."

"I'd like to continue working here too," Skylar said. "I'd also like to join Braden and Hugh. If that's okay?" she asked Braden.

"Sure," he agreed readily.

Courtney looked at them. "We'll start over and work through this. Your employment is not contingent on studying the Bible with Hugh, though. Remember that."

They both smiled at each other and Alex and Courtney. "Thank you," they said in unison.

"Expect to work hard because we only have a short time before Paul's wedding to get everything ready," Courtney said. "Welcome to the staff of Crocus Hill Inn."

CHAPTER 53

Sunday morning, Courtney woke to the smell of bacon. Alex was cooking her favorite breakfast: eggs, bacon, and pancakes.

After her shower, she greeted him with a kiss in the kitchen. "Thanks for cooking for me this morning. You did as much cleaning as I did Friday afternoon and Saturday. You must be tired."

After turning the burner down on the stove, he stepped over to where she stood by the island and pulled her into his arms. "I slept well last night. The relief of having Phil's death solved and having you near me helped me relax. How about you?" He looked down into her face.

"I didn't even hear you get up or shower this morning. That should tell you something." She returned his hug, and then he moved away to check on the food.

"Almost done. I need to flip these pancakes. You can take the pan from the oven with the others staying warm."

When she opened the oven door, she laughed as the stack of pancakes nearly toppled over. She carefully carried the pan over to the table, where Alex had already set a potholder for it. He'd also set out the orange juice, butter, syrup, and dishes.

She thanked God for Alex. Staring at him, she admired his sunny smile and strong hands making her a meal.

"I'm hungry," he said.

And she thanked God the week passed somewhat successfully despite Phil's death. She figured she'd never see most of their guests again, except Melanie. She planned to return and work on her feelings over her husband's death.

"We did it, Alex," she said as he carried a plate of bacon and bowl of scrambled eggs to the table.

He placed a hand on her shoulder and squeezed. "You sure did." He went to get the last of the pancakes.

She sat down and watched him, feeling the warmth of his hand on her shoulder. She was so blessed. "I can't believe our opening week is over. It certainly didn't match anything I imagined."

He sat down beside her and took her hand. "How could we have even thought of Phil's death? Let's pray and then do a postmortem."

"Funny." She bowed her head and hid her smile at his silly pun. "God. Thank you for the blessing of this food, especially the massive pile of pancakes. I will be doing justice to your bounty. Thank you also for my wonderful husband, Alex, for his understanding and being a perfect mate for me. We're grateful the innocent have been spared this week, and we ask for your grace and forgiveness for Lucy as she struggles to work through the coming weeks."

When she paused, Alex said, "And thank you, God, for my wonderful wife, who has a caring and sincere heart to help others. Please bless both of us as we continue to work for the good of our guests here at Crocus Hill Inn. Amen."

"Amen," Courtney echoed before turning to him. "I feel like I have so many things to be grateful for, I could spend all day thanking God."

"Me too. Right now, these pancakes." He speared some and put them on his plate.

Courtney pulled the bowl of eggs closer and scooped up a healthy portion. "We have two weeks now until the wedding to get this place ready. Mainly the landscaping. What do you think?"

"We'll get it done." He laughed. "I've had a few texts from volunteers already. They'll come out and help me get the deck up, clean up the backyard, and plant a few bushes. Between the volunteers, Braden, and myself, you'll blink, and the magic will have happened."

"How did you get volunteers? We didn't ask anyone for help, did we?" She frowned down at her bacon, confused by the outpouring of help. Not that Elm City residents hadn't been willing to assist them. They supported the efforts to get Crocus Hill Inn going since they'd heard about it.

Alex swallowed his food. "They want the inside story of this past week. We'll be getting questions thrown at us after church this evening. Politely, of course."

Courtney's confusion cleared. "Ah. Let's enjoy their help and keep most of the details to ourselves."

"Agreed."

They settled on the couch after breakfast, snuggling together and enjoying being with each other. "It's so nice to not have any guests to cater to." Courtney let out a breath. "Peace and quiet."

"I know." His arm surrounded her. "Are you sorry you started the inn? Do you want to quit?"

She snuggled closer. "Bite your tongue, Mr. Richmond. This is my dream, and I love it. We're going to run into problems, but hopefully no more dead bodies."

"No more dead bodies. We'll be celebrating Paul and Hannah's wedding in a few weeks. That should be safe enough."

She kissed him on the chin. "Nobody but your brother, his bride-to-be, and our family and friends. I'm looking forward to the festive event. I can't wait for them to get here. What could possibly be dangerous with them?"

~~~

Join Courtney and Alex for their next adventure in *The Last Cake*.

Picture of Book 3 – The Last Cake
~~~

https://www.jeanrezab.com

ACKNOWLEDGMENTS

Considerable thanks to my family who encouraged me in my writing journey.

Thank you to Sally, Ruth, and Connie, great friends who also are terrific at keeping me motivated to continue writing. I couldn't have finished this book without your support. Also, thanks to my writing friend, Jann, who keeps me on track.

Special thanks to the excellent editor, Krista Venero, at Mountains Wanted Publishing & Indie Author Services for great suggestions. She helped create a better book than I could have envisioned on my own.

Thank you to the book cover designer at Sunset Rose Books for an amazing cover.

Also by Jean_Rezab

Crocus Hill Inn Mysteries
The Last Owners
The Last Scam
The Last Cake

Richmond Sibling Series
Chokecherry Valley Comfort
Chokecherry Valley Joy
Chokecherry Valley Love
Chokecherry Valley Faith
Chokecherry Valley Collection

Standalones
In This Place Together (Biblical)
The Prediction (Mystery)

ABOUT THE AUTHOR

Jean Rezab writes from her home in North Dakota. She loves the wide-open prairie and spring wildflowers. She's an avid mystery reader. An excerpt of her work has appeared in ND Humanities Magazine.

Visit her website https://www.jeanrezab.com